Kenyon Boltz

Ted Gerencser

Black Rose Writing

www.blackrosewriting.com

ISBN: 978-1-935605-40-9

PUBLISHED BY BLACK ROSE WRITING

www.blackrosewriting.com

Printed in the United States of America

The Unanswered Dreams of a Dead Man is printed in 12-point Book Antiqua

Cover illustrated by Joe Romano II

www.joeromano2.blogspot.com

6/30/10

"To all the people who said I couldn't, thank you."

—Kenyon Boltz

*"I dedicate this to St. Therese of Lisieux.
She's the reason I was born."*

— Ted Gerencser

FOR
MR. + MRS. LEECH
WHAT GREAT
NEIGHBORS
WHAT GREAT
KIDS.

Ted

CHAPTER 1

THE REASON BEHIND THE REASON

Burning yourself, be it a hot pan, or a flame, is a taut lesson in the humanly order we occupy amongst ourselves. Many, if not almost all, in the throes of youth and virility, think they are invincible, immortal, if not wholeheartedly entitled to long age. I was in this camp without as much as a change of clothes; just got in the car, rolled down the windows, cranked the radio to music and lyrics bashing the conventionality of stiff upper-lipped curmudgeons.

But, laying in this person's yard, one night after parking my car at the end of his driveway along a deserted road in the backwoods of Medina County, OH, I was awoken to the vibe of flashing red and blue, being accosted by the men in blue for allegedly driving drunk. I would have gone down for my third and lengthy rehabilitation in the service of the state if it wasn't for an old man coming down the driveway saying I was in his company the entire night and my car was driven by somebody else: a friend of his, who blocked him in since they argued over who won at their last game of chess.

The officers looked at each other with dire angst because they knew the story was not the honest one. Unapologetic, they released me to his custody and went their way. And there I was, swaying in the night wind, covered by the thinning foliage of his canopy of trees, standing in front of this stoic, spire of a man, defined not just in lines cracking his aged skin, but in his superior posture.

I grossly thanked him with a nod, receiving only a curt

snort and him walking his long driveway to the only light emitting through the trees. I followed since his door was left open. I entered watching him turn a corner to a larger room. He sat down in his favorite chair, seeing that it was the only chair in this vaulted ceiling loft. He pointed to his liquor cabinet and I thankfully nodded and served myself.

When you look at linchpins or crossroads, one could not be as significant and wavering than to stand in this room, holding a gin and tonic, fireplace active with subtle flames, and his phonograph playing Beethoven, or maybe Ravel. His name is Ted Christopher, acquired simply by reading a letter on top of his liquor cabinet. He then pointed to the kitchen to grab a chair and place it directly opposite him, breaking the room into a dual dichotomy of him and the fireplace, me and the phonograph.

I sat sipping my drink but finished it so unabashedly quick, I fixed myself another drink. I noticed his drink was not empty... yet, so I went back to my place, the chair across from him. My eyes kept darting around while he stared off my shoulder at a picture of a young child standing at the end of a pier. I stared at it myself, wondering what the child was looking at. The second drink was finished.

"You all right, kid?"

"Yeah, hate these headaches you get-"

"You'll be alright. Just choke down another drink... You know, you are the first person in a decade to be here, inside my sanctuary."

"I guess... thank you?"

"Don't thank me just yet. Not yet. All in due time."

The night crept on with out much more except for a couple more drinks for himself and me passing out in the chair, falling to the floor and noticing he was gone. I took his chair and fell asleep.

I got up with the sun illuminating the clear August sky.

I briefly looked for him, but left without much effort or pursuit. I entered my car and sat there for a second studying the area: a unique niche of a house living amongst the trees with a distinguishing '234' by the overhead of the front door. I leave.

It was approximately 10 days when I drove back late at night to this place. Did not pull into his driveway but blocked it in the same, mistaken manner as before. Maybe as some way to spark his memory of who I was; I had no idea that returning would be forever returning, absorbing, listening, escaping, and journeying amidst the remnants of this man's life. I couldn't stop; I didn't want to stop. It was a quenching drink of ice-cold soul. Too bad nobody knew anything and didn't listen before. My treat.

Nothing stirs the internal drive we all serve, or we all hibernate to, than a curiosity and a mystery. My free time has run up and my visits have spilled over into responsibility time, which has been shoveled away to pursue this enigma of a man in nature. I haven't told my friends or family about him; I feel privileged, privy to have this wealth of possibility, potential: especially when nothing has been served up for an easy sail upon my life or future up-bringing.

Not to be a whiner or a prankster of cynicism, I find this new event to be more engrossing than hanging at a bar or pub, slamming several pints coupled with a large amount of 'what-if' conversations and 'would you do her' kind of games.

On an average Saturday morning to the laymen, I found the peculiar silence in his backyard woods to be of complete solace and serenity. I stood and stared into the brush until the lines blurred into a soup of earth tones and shapes. That blurring of definition and expectations from perception is important. Today, he sends me out to dig up this poem or song he sharply instructed to find. I say poem but he says song; I do not argue with him. I simply nod; I do not want to irritate him. He is volatile; it must be his lengthy fermenting by himself.

The map was drawn out by hand; the directions are vague: the innumerable possibilities, the waste of time, but I feel time is non-existent, non-threatening in this search. Quite a lesson into the potency of living life now versus planning or scheduling ahead; so I venture straight from the steps of his back door and head directly to a broken tree, one that must have been destroyed by a singular strike of lightning. The trunk gnarled and knotted, split down the middle with the lush leaves long dead. From there, I turn down-stream from the near creek.

I come upon another tree matching the previous marker and begin to dig with my hands, than opt for a rock. I dig possessed; one foot below I see a band from a zip bag used for fruit or meat in the fridge and instantly think how well this has lasted underneath ground. Maybe the company should add this to their marketing campaign.

I sit on the bank overlooking the curve of the stream leading deeper into the woods and open the bag. A smell of clay, mud, and dampness permeates from the paper, unraveling the hand-written piece of notebook paper. It was definitely an original copy. Not done with a computer or even a typewriter. It was hand-written and the paper was old parchment, maybe even papyrus: I forgot to pay attention in class that day. It was dutifully titled "This Life Unknown". I read.

THIS LIFE UNKNOWN

I'm coming down
Coming down

Into a wilderness
That is unexplained
But explained

I have seen
A life between
Heaven and hell
Where nature sings

A glorious tune
Of our existence
{The sound of nature and music comes to a halt}

ARE YOU HERE?

Do you know the answers?
Do you ask the questions?
In this life -- This life unknown

I was born
Full of hope
Full of glory

I was loved
Nurtured to believe

I could change
(Everything)
I could be
(Anything)
I could
(Make it better)

In this life unknown
Seeing what the world has shown
In this life unknown

{The sound of nature and music comes to a halt}

ARE YOU HAPPY?

Do you live
Beneath blue skies?

Do you focus
On what's inside?

In this life
This life unknown

{The sound of nature and music comes to a halt}

Broken branches
Lingering over head
Pathways misleading
The thought I have –are unread
Where do you go
When you're dead?

[Solo Thoughts]
In this life unknown
I took a walk
By myself
Through the fields
To find myself
In the woods
Searching
For a place
I could exist

And be free
From all the trouble
I see
On the outside
I try
To understand why

We haven't grown
In this life unknown.

I sit quiet and let the words flow through my nerves and track the entry into my brain to release to my skin. I think about the path I walked in the woods. I think about the sun setting before my eyes. I think about my own life, specific nuggets, such as the time I woke up from a pool party before anyone else and watched the shimmering slants of the pool in its slumber for an awfully long time.

I walk with the paper up-stream, back to the man, Ted Christopher. I pondered on the amount of time this manuscript stayed unheard, buried beyond ears and conversation. I sweep across the entire landscape around me and think of the hundreds or thousands that may lay hidden, given to the earth instead of shared with thousands. This makes me laugh; who would dig up every single one? No one has time.

I get back to the house with a looming darkness battling a half moon rising to this occasion. Something to the side of his overgrown brick patio entices me to further look. I try not to waver from direct routes that he tells me for a relapse in what he is doing, thinking; I have to be honest with myself, this old guy may have some loot and no one to leave it to.

The object turns out to be a fire-pit with a large pile of ashes, not charcoal or wood, but... paper. A couple of burnt edges with some minute writing but I can't make out anything, except 'This Life'. As a writer, you have to be real disgruntled or ingenious to just simply torch what is not needed at the precise time. I still have papers from freshman year in high school.

I enter the main room with the same set-up: him in his cushion chair like an old tycoon and a blanket with the fire going and then my ridiculously uncomfortable kitchenette chair.

CHAPTER 2

IS ART CONSIDERED ART BY MERE PERFORMANCE?

"I found what you sent me for."

"I can't remember- what song is that?"

"This Life Unknown."

He springs up the quickest I've seen so far, fetching another drink of top shelf whiskey, but can't read the label. He laughs clumsily.

"I wrote that in high school – I was 16. Life back then was simple. I wrote so much stupid shit. I guess it doesn't matter."

"So, then why send me out in the middle of nowhere?"

Returning to his chair cautiously, he grimaces, then relaxes: no answer. I sit down across him leaning intently on my words.

"It does matter. Where are the rest of the poems, or songs?"

He rubs his tired eyes, fishing for his melting ice-cubes in the glass.

"I know where they are. It's not often you are asked to resurrect things you desired buried."

I shoot the rest of my drink; the liquor goes well when inside his house. A moment of silence: broken by his cough.

"Tonight, a journey. Walk past the shed in the east corner of the yard and find the path. On that path, you will come to a tree, a pine tree in the middle of the maple forest. The path here will split into two. This is not a Robert Frost poem, moron. Just choose the path on the right. It will lead you to the bank on the stream, guiding you to a huge, misplaced boulder. What a great platform to cast a line and maybe catch a perch or insight. Well... do what you can to move that rock, because underneath that rock and a little beneath the earth is a wooden box. It's getting late, the night owl will be watching. Go in the drawer, next to the kitchen sink and grab a flashlight."

I look at him dumb-founded, a wide-eyed deer; he continues gesturing for me to go as if mesmerized, completely lost in his thought. He doesn't respond again. I finish my drink and do what I am told.

The darkness I enter is canvassing the ominous forest to an abyss. The night creatures tweet, crick, and fizzle around. The bohemian life of fire-flies offers a rhythmic glow to a night harmony I don't comprehend or wish to. The clean air heightens my senses against the relaxing flow of drink in my blood. I hear each crinkle and crack of leaves and twigs with each step. The distinguishing cone of light from the flashlight acts as a saber, slicing my way this and that way. I am surprised by my actions and motivation. I am a loner except for a few close friends. Solitude is not a lonely place for me. I find solace within myself even though I am told and prodded by others to go out more often and be with people my age. It is all bunk; this is more alive than I have been in months.

After locating the shed, I continue on but stop short. I go back to the side and attempt to peer in the shed's pane. The light can not pierce the grime and dirt from years upon years of build-up. The door has a new padlock on it; I walk on disappointed with my saber.

The boulder is large and irregular; a slight growth of moss covers the base making it quite slippery. I hunch down, put my shoulder down and push! Nothing. I get better position and a large stick to act as a lever while pushing. Slow, budging, the suction of the earth and rock releases the vacuum seal and it rolls to its side, its flat side. It appears that this might have been the original place of the rock. I dig with ease and find the wooden box. I pull it out and inspect: a homemade box with a door hinge for the connection. A rough-shot style of make but a tight seal no less. I want to open it here.

I make it back to the house; my cell phone rings. I ignore it and go inside. The old man is not in his chair so I place the box down by his chair and quickly make a drink. I have just noticed that the liquor is restocked. There is no cabinet or any place to keep it in the room. Old man's got a stash, may have to see if I could score a couple of bottles. I walk around the room with no new discoveries so I venture to the kitchen. The place is hospital clean with a hint of strong cleanser odor. Nothing on the counter tops, no pots and pans hanging, nothing in the sink: it's like he rents this empty place. I dare not search through his cabinets because, to be honest, I don't care, like most others if they were in this situation would probably pull a Hardy Boys and investigate. The drink is flowing again.

Back in the main room, I check out the missed call: a girl I've been trying to stay in touch with but, alas, only mild success. The whole half-country distance can be a deterrent both emotionally and obviously physically. I wonder why I attract to women I can't-

SLAM!

Ted Christopher has returned with an arrogant entrance to frighten me. He walks with ease to his chair. For his senior age, he moves Spartan-like and concise, the dim lighting of the fire disguises and offers illusion to how old he really is.

"Damn good with directions, back sooner than I expected."

"Call it curiosity mixed with alcohol: a fabulous cocktail."

"Yes, alcohol… I see you have made quite a dent in my stock."

He turns the bottles of his liquor so the labels are not visible. I flounder.

"Well, I-"

"Who gives a shit, take a seat; relax."

We both sit in silence.

"Well are you going to stare at the fucking box or are you going to open it?"

In the box rests a school bag with a stack of papers wrapped tightly in plastic. I rip through the plastic and discover about 15 poems.

"Go ahead, open one up and read."

"It's dark, I can't-"

"What do you want me to do, light a fucking candle? You have a flashlight."

I turn it on and read-

"Stop! Read it out loud."

I shrug from his insistence.

I AM HAPPY

(slow)
Everyone around me
Seems happy
Is everyone –pretending
Just acting
Around me
(fast)
I can't even write
Can't even say
What it is… that I feel

I don't even know
Sometimes don't even care
Whether or not... it is real
(slow)
For I spent my whole life
Trying to figure it out
And what it is
I don't know
(slower)
I don't know
(fast)
Is this how it is
Is this how it was meant to be
All this time
Thinking I was free
Trying to believe
(slow)
Mother – Father
Do you love me?

I'm sorry
(fast)
Was it one decision
That changed my outcome
Or a series of events
That changed what I have become
(slow)
I don't know
What it is
I don't know
(fast)
Did I miss the path
Did I make a wrong turn
Is it too late to go back
What is it that I yearn
(slow)
I don't know
(slower)
I spent my whole life
Trying to figure it out
And finally

I figured it out
(even slower)
I am acting
Just pretending
Around you
I am happy

I shut the flashlight off. His gaze drifts away.

"High School: back then it was easy. It just made sense. Yes, like any other teenager, I felt lost, but now, when I look back upon it… I wasn't. I was just naive."

"Nothing wrong with being naïve."

"No… and yes. I can't put a finger on it. Maybe it was the raging hormones, the animal desires. Maybe it was just being afraid to scratch the surface, to be alive; you know, create a heartbeat."

"I'm curious, why you sharing these poems? Why now? Why dig'em up?"

"Not everything needs a reason."

I glance back at the poem and linger on the tempo.

"You could probably have this performed."

"Don't be stupid. It's not that easy. The obvious is not so obvious. Do you feel that you know something that I do not? If so, then you are smarter than I am."

My blood pressure rises. I sit and read it again, hovering over the series of events versus one decision. I calm down. It felt like seconds but must have been minutes since he was passed out. I knew something inside me just knew to stay. I sat in the corner and turned on the flashlight. I read "Life."

LIFE

So much pain
Yet so much joy
So much sorrow
Yet so much happiness

So much sadness
Yet so much hope
So much agony
Yet so much passion

So much madness
Yet so much clarity
So much hate
Yet so much love

FOR LIFE

So much anger
Yet so much excitement
So much fear
Yet so much
Bravery

So much failure
Yet so much success
So much heartache
Yet so much pleasure

So much hurt
Yet so much desire
So much... So much
To honor

Life.

I ran my hand through my hair as I walked by him. He held his drink like a pro. His posture and stoic expression in sleep lingers with me as I walk through his corridor; I notice a classic gold leaf frame encapsulating a family photo: five young women and a young man. I exit his house. I surprise myself with the act of asking myself if I will be back.

CHAPTER 3

TO SLEEP – TO LET GO – TO DIE

It's been about a week since leaving his place that night. I awake for the first time and the first thought of the day was about going back. The boomerang of the time wasted to time gained cycles rapidly, for I knew what I know, and the words read have made their mark. Then the musical argument inside my head builds to a fond crescendo pitch that says 'Yes, you will be there tonight.' Aside from my slow awakening, I shake it off with a quick laugh and head to work. I'll shower tomorrow.

Work: it does not begin in the office, at my desk, or with the first phone call, it begins as such: unlock car, place coffee so it doesn't spill, light a smoke, adjust radio, seatbelt locked, reverse, stoplight, traffic, two sudden brake jobs, a nodding of the head of "why?", finding a spot, noticing you can squeeze one more smoke in, smiling the empty hellos, turning on computer, 30 minutes of internet, a walk around the office, couple of hours of work, a snack, a bathroom break, lunch inside my car, back to desk, a cup of coffee for the ever-invigorating second half of the day, 2 hours of work, a break of internet searching, a small amount of calendar planning, and redundant talk with co-workers. Clock out. This is American Productivity at its purest and truest.

The time before heading to the old man's house is a smear: no definitive action or event that can engross my divided attention. If words can have a shaman effect or any residual mark, I thirst for more. On the way, I passed one of my favorite parks where many nights with flings, friends, strangers, have gone down with such motley results. I stand outside in silence and have a smoke with a steady gaze up into the sky, to the stars, to the moon, for the moment of clarity to hit me like space junk from a weather satellite crashing into me. No such event... this time.

I pull into his driveway normal instead of parking sideways as previously. I don't think Ted Christopher has a car; if he did, probably a jalopy beyond repairing. He's got to have family around here or assisted living maybe, maybe not out of dementia or physical ability but because he is lazy and finds it suiting for someone else to move for him. I would probably be that guy some day.

Something about arriving in the precursor of midnight makes the anticipation pop. At least he has drink. A sticky note on the door: Come in. A simple statement on the front door provides a sensational effect of progress being made to a greater good.

As I enter, I am floored by the thunderous volume of Nessun Dorma, sung by Pavarotti. This is the one quality a house secluded from others has: music as loud as your equipment allows. The song echoes in his foyer, the framed picture on the wall rattles, I enter the main room to feel vibrations bombarding my body, entering my cells, and mutating my DNA. The song ends with the small buzz of decibels too loud. Laughter follows from Ted.

"No one shall sleep... a perfect title wouldn't you say? Come. Get a drink. So what did you do today?"

"The same routine of being mediocre in my paint-by-number schema. I could go into detail but I think I would cry since I will be lamenting Monday."

Raw laughter blankets the room: irritating.

"Why are you laughing?"

"I'm laughing because I think you don't have a clue. Not just by what you say, but by what you do. You, like most Americans, wake up and work. One day, you will be on your death bed and you will wonder why. You know what, it doesn't matter. Grab that old book bag of mine from the corner and unzip the front pocket."

I open the front pocket and find a 5x7 frame of a young girl and a guy on prom night, face to face, in each other's arms, smiling with genuine chemistry.

"Just set it on the mantle."

I dust off the mantle and set it down.

"You knew I would be here, didn't you?"

He sits down and gets comfortable.

"I used to be your age. You had a couple of days of lingering thoughts, a couple more days of apprehension, and then the confrontation in your mind. Curiosity is a funny thing; it killed the cat you know."

The fireplace crackles and pops.

"Search the book bag and find a song titled 'Faraway'.

I search the bag and find the song; the fire is bright, warm. I don't need the flashlight.

"Stop and look at the picture."

I stare at her intently: her presence cannot be argued. Ted clears his throat.

"It's my girl, my high school sweetheart. She was beautiful that night, her heart pure. I want you to know that about her. What an angel. I had no idea what I was doing. She was a virgin, a good girl. She looked at me that night and knew that I knew. Her eyes were innocent. She just smiled and said, 'Ted—I love you'. God, I miss her."

I read the song out loud, starting with the title.

FARAWAY

Slipping through… into my arms
Feeling secure… within my hands
Making you safe… in my touch
Bringing you in… into my reach

I am holding you tight
Never letting you go
Faraway

Moving your head back
Exposing your neck
Feeling your heartbeat
Within each breath

I am holding you tight
Never letting you go
Faraway

Looking into your eyes
Reaching pass the surface
Drifting into your soul
Slowly losing control

Of everything
That is around us
In everything
That confines us
-To this place
Where there is only us
And I love us

I am holding you tight
Never letting you go
Faraway.

Ted Christopher

I finish and linger on the last stanza. I see his name but no date; I assume it was written a long time ago; however, it exudes freshness, as if written yesterday. I wonder. Ted pours another drink of scotch and water. He hands me the glass.

"Scotch and water- classy guy... Was it love?"

I look back at the photo on the mantle.

"This photo, this memory, these words- kept for so long can only bring regret and perhaps self-loathing."

I can tell I hit a cord; he takes his time pouring himself a scotch and water.

"No, don't ever assume. Yes, I do regret some of my decisions. But it's part of life and you have to move on. Was it right? Was it wrong? I'm not sure."

He looks out the window and stares at the moon.

"I could have married her. She could have borne my children, whom may have borne more children."

He sits down in his leather seat and drinks, aggressively shaking the cubes of ice in his glass.

"You have no idea who we were, who I am. Do you even know what it's like to love?"

I take a deep breath. I actually think hard of that question so bluntly placed in front of me as a hunter with his carcass; I abruptly flash back to the conversation.

"Okay, I apologize, but what is there for me, personally, to gain from this… this… manifesto of innocence gained?"

He laughs.

"Kid, you kill me, precisely everything. You are witnessing words of ecstasy, youth, and virginity given, words that can be placed into a tangible world to be analyzed and scrutinized by public opinion. Words to be held, heard, shared, improved upon… and most importantly, revised."

"But they were buried."

"Yes, they were. You are a smart cookie. The time was not right. The world was not ready. It's like when somebody you know dies, you get sad, but in time you realize without maybe even realizing the difference that person made on your own life. Just think of a knife- the more you use it, the duller it becomes; but sharpen the knife constantly and put it away until you need- must have it, it will cut and cut deep, down the spine and leave its mark... ... on the reader."

"Shit, I don't know if you're brilliant or if you lost your mind. Do you think your high school sweetheart still reminisces?"

He goes back to the phonograph, smiling, and puts 'Nessun Dorma' back on ear-splitting volume. I relax against the wall with a drink. My routine of work does not enter my thoughts, only virgins in white, flowing dresses, senior prom, and people, friends, and my high school sweetheart drunk on laughter and bliss.

The grating skips from the phonograph insidiously knocking me from my trance; Ted Christopher has disappeared. My drink must have spilled throughout the euphoric transcendence of the song and my visions. Time for another drink... and maybe another poem...?

I peer into the book bag and catch on a torn-up sheet, like it was stuffed in haste. I read it by the fire, aloud-

WORDS

Paint my portrait
With black and white chalk
Blend in colors of yellow and red-
To symbolize hope and despair
Black-out the sun
And dry out the river
Deaden the flowers
And crumble the mountains

Black-out the moon
And shoot at the stars
For my life... is insignificant.

Infect the canvas
With soulless creatures
Take charcoal
And light a match

Watch the living room; burn
The furniture; in flames
The grandfather clock; chimes
As a women in red; enters

She watches in delight
As ink, drips from my tired eyes
Her delicate fingers
Wipe away my tears
Her long dark hair
Shadows my existence
As she says...
Your life... is insignificant

The portrait and the man
Welt away – in the flames
The women in red and the audience
Seem happy and clap
For the story of this life
And ultimately this death
Was an experiment
Of how America
Perceives
Art.

These... these re-collections, musings, introspections, pontifications, I do not know what to do, when to absorb, incorporate, such peculiar, possibly nutritional lessons for the mind, as opposed to the Burger King I see and hear everyday. How can such self-indulgent confidence run rampant through this man's veins, coursing each second, in/out, of his heart and not wonder why no one is here to wallow in his cantankerous tenacity? I am not evil, but I am contemptuous toward these... people. I think it's time for me to leave.

Upon reaching the door, I do a double-take to the far wall, a gleam, reflection, outside the eye: a crucifix, outlaid in gold trim, creamy pearl. How did I not see that before?

SLAM!

I fucking literally jump out of my skin. A bible has just crashed to the floor with a sticky note attached to the cover.

"Nice one, asshole, scared the shit out of me!"

I bend down; the note reads 'Psalm 23 – good luck'. I exit the house with the bible underneath my arm, a Tom Collins glass in my hand and a silky, full moon above, to guide my drive on this perfect witching night in Ohio.

CHAPTER 4

IN SIGHT OF THE FUTURE

I run into my place, toss keys to the floor, turn on a light, place the bible on my only table and pace. It's late and I have a meeting tomorrow morning early. A meeting: foolish activity with foolish lip service amounting to foolish effects. I turn on my computer and peruse around for one of my last rants that I will bring to him, to show him how such random wanderings can cause a simple stroll to morph into a virile, vociferous boast of contempt and cynicism. *Psalm 23...* *Psalm 23...* reverberates in my cavernous mind. I stop and glance over to the curled note on the bible cover. Seconds slog by like sewage. The game of pong plays in my head, myself moving the smaller paddle, wildly, trying to keep up with the speed of a racing mind: I lose. I walk to the couch and pick up the bible and open to-

Psalm 23

A psalm of David.

1 The LORD is my shepherd, I shall not be in want.
2 He makes me lie down in green pastures, he leads me beside quiet waters,
3 He restores my soul. He guides me in paths of righteousness for his name's sake.
4 Even though I walk through the valley of the shadow of death, I will fear no evil, for you are with me; your rod and

your staff, they comfort me.
5 You prepare a table before me in the presence of my
enemies. You anoint my head with oil; my cup overflows.
6 Surely goodness and love will follow me all the days of my
life, and I will dwell in the house of the LORD forever.

I read with the utmost interest and reverence but I can't get into this earthly divinity style, not now: the petulant tumor of love lost is too much in my recent past to easily, smoothly transit to the pious and penitent. The booze is making me tired, tired to combat strategically against vice and virtue. I... I... just don't know. I lie down on the couch and take a long look at the ceiling. The shadows from the outside lamps present a tapestry of myriad shades in degrees of black: my soul personified on the ceiling; Sleep lures my eyes to shut comfortably.

I walk cautiously, to a center spotlight, narrowed to a stool. Everything is enveloped in darkness. I sit down. With a mechanical thrust and spark, the lights thunder on. The 16 foot lighting grid and catwalk above me illuminate a studio space with 8 varying, stage sets placed in an octagon: I am the center.

A shadow of a man above me is navigating the path of the spotlight; my eyes vicariously follow as if I am under a musical trance. I can hear a faint audio track of mild tempo, acoustic music stylized with a female's velvet voice crooning. The lyrics are jumbled.

Suddenly,

16 people, 8 boys, 8 girls, in various outfits, walk out in two-by-two fashion. They all share the same realm of age: high school.

Each couple walks to their respective set and seamlessly prepare as if a director was waiting. The spotlight shoots to the set directly in front of me, 12 o'clock position.

A boy leans casually against a locker, eyes locked on his

female's eyes as they get ready to leave, walking side by side in the school hallway.

The spotlight takes my eyes to the exact opposite side; I spin around to the 6 o'clock position.

The couple stands at odds from each other; a heated argument ensues inside a hallway; no one is around. The boy leaves throwing his hands up; the girl slides down the lockers in slow tears, sadness.

The spotlight goes to the 10 o'clock position.

A girl and boy walk to a swing set on a playground and begin swinging slowly, laughing, kicking up mulch as they leisurely spin and twirl, bumping into each other.

The spotlight goes to 4 o'clock position.

-   The couple is standing underneath a tree: the guy is trying to console the crying girl but she pushes him away in complete, utter anger. His face is awash in fear, concern. Her facial reactions portray disappointment; she storms off, leaving the boy to put his hand on the tree for support as his head hangs low.

The spotlight goes to 8 o'clock position.

- The girl sits on the sidelines of a football game: it has just ended, the boy comes over, takes off his helmet and gives her a kiss and a hug. He holds the game ball in the air.

The spotlight goes to 2 o'clock position

- The girl awaits her boy as he comes off the field but is ignored when a cheerleader comes running up to him and seductively flirts with him; she watches with a sunken heart.

The spotlight goes to 9 o'clock position.

The boy and girl slowly enter bed and methodically caress each other. The girl is nervous, unsure, she feebly tries to enjoy the guy's hands on her. He smiles at her; she smiles back. They embrace into one naked body.

The spotlight goes to 3 o'clock position.

The boy and girl sit at a kitchen table across from each

other with a divider between them in the form of a pregnancy test. She picks it up and stares at the boy with a blank look on her face. His face is ravenously thirsty for an answer.

THUM! Lights out on everything, spotlight is back on top of me, the music has turned into a volatile mix of drums, bass, and guitar, heavy-metal fills the studio space to ear-splitting level. An omnipotent voice breaks the music to a repetition of "Fall Into Me...Fall Into Me...". The spotlight begins to fade, as I fall off the stool-

I awake in the morning with a start. I look around in feverish manner: what, where, who... The TV is on a music video of heavy metal, my computer is on, the window is open, and papers are all over the floor. I look at my watch. I'm late for the meeting. I catch a last glance in my place at the note on the bible: Psalm 23.

My Friday night is here; usually empty rambling of straying here or there. I decide to drive to his house. Before I leave, I print off a page from my computer and lock up. The walk to my car has a wind caress that is simply the epitome of nature's body kiss. It is a humid, significantly bright dusk in late August. My dream kept me pre-occupied at work today. It was vivid; it was poignant; it was... not me in those unfair arrangements: as if I was sitting off-stage as a contributor, a script consultant to a phantom motion picture. I drift in and out of contemplation as my skills go into auto-pilot while I categorize, forcefully squint in order to get a better remembrance of their faces, making sure they weren't me and my high school sweetheart. They can't be! I never played high school football, I played soccer and wrestled. I pass a public library and almost cause a collision because I need to do some research on this dude. His words are kindling distant embers to burn again; I shudder at the thought of the re-kindling if this is true. Some things are best left buried, seriously.

CHAPTER 5

SIMPLY BEING SIMPLE

His front door is wide open, to not just me, but to any and all creatures: yes, I have to get to a library and research; too radical, too eclectic not to. The smell of incense is strong and musky; its translucent tail leads me up the stairs near the foyer to a loft. He sits alone in a lounge chair, staring out a bay window overlooking the serene woods where his plot co-exists. The high school book bag dangles from a single hook on the wall. It is carpeted, pristine, as if this was the first time entered. I notice I have a better chair to sit on than the stupid kitchenette chair. I noisily approach.

"You know you left the door wide open."

"I have nothing to be afraid of. Don't sit. No time to waste today."

He hands me two loose sheets of notebook paper and stands up and stares out the window. I look at him and wonder what he gazes at or sees, even thinks.

"I'm too old, but I can still see the forest; I am too old to walk the damn path. Take the two songs and walk the path you can see here from this window. Sit at the edge of the bank and take off your shoes. Dangle your feet in the water and feel the sunlight upon your face."

I hesitate, but eventually abide and leave his house, walking the path. My mind is completely vacant except for the action of my walk and the innate sense of direction. I reach the destination and do as I am told. I take off my shoes and socks and dip my feet in the cool, grey stream;

acknowledging the sunlight with a closure of my eyes.

The warm sensation eels through my skin and fills my body with a silent energy of true conformation. I take a few, deep breaths and read the first song-

OUT OF A WINDOW

Out of a window... a child sees the world
Through the fields, beyond the ocean... he stares
At a life, he dreams of... in the clear

I see him there
Locked away (in his own room)
With no place to go

Out of a window... the child leaps
Into the leaves... he falls, to the top of the hill... he goes
To lie upon the grass, beneath the stars... he shines

I see him there
Locked away (in his own world)
With no place to go

Out of a window... snow falls upon the field
Where streams freeze over, to a time of spring
Where leaves come into bloom and the sun comes up too soon.

I see it there
Out of my reach
I see it there
Trying to teach
Trying to teach

I look to my feet beneath the surface: the flesh ripples in the creek. His words are unassuming and grandiose; they are crystals, dirty but shine once cleaned: I do not know how to use them, manipulate them, or name them. These poems

35

must parallel in some enigmatic way, somehow. I get flustered by my extreme concentration in forcing the answer, an answer. I shake my head and move on to the next one; this time, I read aloud-

THE END OF SPRING

Green field
Sunrise
A site of her
Blue eyes

It's like ocean water
It's a sapphire stone

I pour a glass of wine
I think
About this unforgettable time

The stars shine
Like a bright light
Grown up
And out of sight

In the end of spring
A child dreams
An old man song
The time between
What was right
And what went wrong

In the end of spring

There were blue skies
And endless days
Where nothing dies
And everything stays

Till the end of spring

(SOLO – THOUGHT)
She dressed up
In a sun dress
She danced around
With her shoes off
She made a smile
With no make-up on
I gave it back
For her hair was down

In the end of spring
A child dreams
An old man song
The time between
What was right
And what went wrong

In the end of spring

The rain fell
The sun set
She left
Without regret

Big sigh: his mentality is avoiding me like a repellant. I am angered... I breathe deeply. I listen to the scene and ask for something, anything- I hold my breath for the next moment. Not even a bird call, a wind, a rustle of leaves- it's as if I was in a vacuum. I take my feet out and aggressively put my socks and shoes on and trudge back to his house. 'What am I doing here' bellows loudly inside. I have other things I could be doing like... like... calling my friends? I check my phone and realize that my last incoming call was from a creditor. The walk back is overshadowed by a huge cloud blocking the sun.

I run up the stairs to his loft; I don't think he's moved except to breathe.

"Not to be rude, but could I get a drink, maybe two before we-"

A wave of his hand intangibly pushes me to fix two tall drinks. I finish, and as I begin to head upstairs, I notice a large amount of mud footprints on his main room carpet. The sheer volume of them begs the question of how many people were in here: were they looking for something, someone? My voluminous movie background sprouts into a tingling sense of higher intrigue and tickling curiosity. I laugh to myself while checking my back pocket for the printed document I brought.

I sit in the chair to his left, facing the bay window, gazing at the tops of the trees to the west side of his house. The sky continues to be blue; the leaves still flow when the wind blows.

"I read your two songs and didn't feel them. I did what you said and I had a quick taste but it went away as quickly as it came."

TC sighs.

"I figured; you may have been woven into society too far. It's sad to hear that, kid."

"Now, wait a minute! I have grasped the high school sweetheart songs and can relate, for my dream was of a perspective like none before. But with the nature ones, the words are empty, shells of exaggeration mounted on platforms of tissue paper. For Christ's sake, I put my feet in a creek which God only knows what the hell was in there."

He stands up from his chair and stretches and sits back down, staring at me.

"I'm sorry, you can't see it, but nature is all around us. It might be your youth. It may just be your wisdom. I am old, yes, but when I was young I had passion. I saw the world for what the world was: green fields, blue skies, mountains, rivers, streams, the ocean, the early morning fog, the night. The world has not changed, it's still the same. Technology, all that shit; doesn't matter. All that matters is who you are in your heart. Did you listen to my instructions and read Psalm 23?"

"Yes… and you didn't instruct me. I chose to read it."

"Hmm."

The silence that followed was similar to my parents finding out I wasn't going to college right after graduating high school. I break the silence.

"So high school for you was the grape's ape, huh?"

He stares at me and goes back to his drink. The non-reaction was affecting me; I don't know this guy but his silence cuts like a fresh sheet of paper. He chuckles; I silently sigh in relief.

"What the fuck is a grape ape? You ask a lot of questions without knowing what you are asking. What a shame."

One drink is finished; onto the next one.

"A shame in what context? You tell me to go into your forest, backwoods, whatever, dig in the ground and dig up your old memories for you and you're telling me I'm a shame? I mean, no disrespect, but, old man, you gotta have something going on in your head that you're not sharing."

"I do."

"Okay."

I scan around the room for any kind of machine that can play music but find none: just a small bookcase with novels sharing encyclopedic book-bindings. Such a minimalist approach to a grandeur home.

"Hey, I brought something myself-"

"How many times did you read Psalm 23?"

"Once, why? Should I keep reading it?"

"Yes. Do not bring that bible back until you have read it twenty-three times."

"Okay, sure. I brought something to share. Do you want another drink?"

He looks forward out his window in solemn peace, declining the drink with a quick shake of the head.

"Great... here it is."

I read out loud.

Vanilla Life

Liberty finds itself neglected
when it has been a core principle
over our progression in history and technology.
The virtues comprising "liberty" are
For health and political gains.

Sex is becoming more disjointed from the pro-creational
Parenting necessity we are built upon,
Erotic nightmares cloud our daily eyelid shows
with a shaking awakening.
The animal within us all is
Starved and treated to a distilled S&M game
Where our prosperity is relying on intelligence and wealth
Growing, mutating... answers are long overdue
Because we hide behind the comfortable lies than harsh truths.

A riddle to this current trend of scarcity.

Increased longevity of health places the burden of values and libertarians.
A ballerina, elegant grace, regal persona, being turned in
For the hyper-kinetic bourgeois,

A person of increasing indifference
With trendy furniture and exotic lattes.
For the love of God is expendable!

Speak communal advantages of authority
Without the sharp divinity of personal liberties,
As the audience listens on their HD channels,
Comment on the beautiful indulgences in the present.

The guilt-free endurance of walking along a stream
Sitting on a park bench with wind blowing through my head
Playing its earth song.

The blue powder of democracy leaves its electronic fingerprint behind.
If only we could embrace our homelessness as an alien's kiss.
Sisters and brothers are lost everyday: where is the pain going?
Two bio-created Prozacs and we're ready to go.
Love secrets... pushed, tied,
And bottled up to wicked proportions.
24 hours is the liberated, spiritual, intelligent, virtuous creature we believe to be.

I finish with a smile. I can't read his reaction. He sits solid as wood. I am anxious and combusting inside, awaiting intently his acceptance of my opposite angle to his-
"What was that?"
I am caught off-guard by his crudeness.
"You speak of cynicism and of plight from these anonymous figures that supposedly generate our agenda to living. You haven't read or opened your ears to any of my words, my songs, my ballads to the soul."
"I find it better to speak truth, realism."

41

"What are you trying to be- Nietzsche? He was a great writer, but never could be understood. His battle of spiritualization versus intelligence: the ever-lasting, ever-flowing and dynamic flux of struggle, loss, and redemption and salvation is carried away with the millions of degrees of peoples' beliefs and norms in their culture. If you have the supreme Belief then what is done when one does not share this same Belief? You attack with violence and either kill or convert."

He finishes his drink, stands, and paces fanatically.

"Radical hostility against sensuality is a primitive symbol of ignorance in the weak and the masses. Is the gap of sensuality being widened in its schism from our real senses in the event to spare others of its romanticism, its folly for childish antics? This is who you want to idolize? Mount up with words, writings, be it your own or others you share affinity. Seclusion is the only other alternative: a life in the woods to yourself and your own devices of the mind, unpolluted and unmolested from the sinewy grasp of corporate capitalism and departmentalization. Thoreau understood. Why pay taxes?"

I am awestruck by the synergy coming from his movements and words versus the elementary level he timidly assumes. I must have hit a nerve.

"Your style leans toward more enemies than friends. Is it because to conquer and decimate, annihilate the futile, is as rewarding as propagandizing our personal message, values and seeding their growth in others so they can mutate, pervert others into a chain linked by misfortune and misunderstandings? Art prevents all this from happening. For art instills beauty, the spirituality of sensuousness, known as love, and proper expression of what life is and what it can be to obtain, a truth to be told."

He sits back down exhausted, just to come at me more.

"Ahh! But what is right and what is wrong? What is good and what is bad? A writer is anyone who writes for the passion of writing. A writer does not need to be paid for what he writes or respected for the ideas and concepts he creates. A writer simply writes for a reader to learn and appreciate their own life. A writer connects with the human condition and emotion. A great writer brings the reader into his world and makes him or her understand something that he or she never quite understood. The writer puts down on paper what a reader can imagine and use to better their own life and future. I'm sorry that you didn't understand why I sent you to the pond. Who knows, ten years from now, you may."

I clink the ice against my glass, subliminally hinting I need to get another drink.

"Get yourself another drink and come back tomorrow night and be ready to spend the night. I need to retire and prepare. You can let yourself out."

He gets up, stops in front of me and puts his hand on my shoulder and stares at my face. He nods in silent approval, and exits down the dark hallway, off the loft and disappears behind the door. The intro to Tchaikovsky's 1812 overture begins to echo throughout the house. I walk down the stairs and notice that the footprints have faded. Was it in my mind? I walk out and close the front door. The thunder of percussion accents my exit.

I reach my car and turn back to the house. The shadows and moonlight carves a dichotic caricature of black and white, a halfway house of totality in abysmal shame versus the virtue in pureness. It is mesmerizing. I don't know what to think anymore. This whole charade is tugging strong on my feeble grasp of reason and emotion. Passion can be deadly in the wrong hands; I'm not so sure if passion is what I need right now. I reverse and leave with the radio off, windows open.

The entire Saturday morning and afternoon was a horrendous soup of painful laziness. My Saturday night should be with friends or a girl, but instead, I walk this country town's main street, passing small family-owned diners, hobby stores, and an out-of-place beautician shop, all closed and empty, contemplating in aggressive football-play mental drawings of X's and O's: go here, then do this, but what happens if this all becomes lost as soon as it materializes inside my mind. The affliction lies not in the old man but what his motive, his secrets, his elusive personality... or maybe in his divine intervention of ending up on his property, about to go down for a long time in state company. All these meanderings loom over my head on this crisp, early September night.

Two tears in a bucket: alas, the confusion of the dream slips in. I stamp it out in anger. I need to know from him. And I need to know now.

I drive like a madman to his place and pass everything in a demonic haste, never blinking or shifting my gaze except for the dead straight laser line of getting to his house. I hit the brakes and skid into his driveway and leap out of the car. I am surprised, literally shocked: his house is lit up, various colors illuminate each room facing the street, music blares from the house. I immediately bring up a psychedelic stereo-type from movies, with hippie chicks, disco and roller skates, cocaine, and... people. I am more excited to see the types of personalities he attracts.

CHAPTER 6

IT'S WHAT HAPPENS WHEN YOU DON'T EXPECT IT TO HAPPEN

Before I get in, a note on the door: ENTER TO TURN IN AND TUNE OUT; I walk the hallway to music playing everywhere, lights carefully placed throughout, and finally, I find a note on the kitchen table: I AM UPSTAIRS MEDITATING, SLEEPING, DREAMING – DON'T BOTHER ME. I drop the note and take a tour in disappointment to see no one except myself. Each room plays a song: first room is "Kashmir" by Led Zeppelin, next, "The End" by The Doors, then "Heroin" by Velvet Underground, and, through the kitchen, in the main room, is "In-A-Gadda-Da-Vida" by Iron Butterfly. I didn't see it the first time but there is writing on the back:

NEXT TO THE DISHWASHER IN THE DRAWER ARE TWO JOINTS. I KNOW YOU HAVE A LIGHTER AND YOU KNOW WHERE THE LIQUOR IS. SMOKE ONE JOINT AND EXPERIENCE EACH ROOM. DO NOT READ THE NOTE IN THE DRAWER UNTIL, AFTER YOU EXPERIENCED EACH ROOM.

I indulge another tour noticing every song is on repeat. A sly thought slides in: where did all this audio equipment come from? Must be from the shed.

What kind of a fool am I to be a part of this? Do drugs, drink, listen to music? I went to high school, college, did that. I'm a working man... what is this dude's bag? I take one joint and go out to his back porch by the fire-pit and light up.

For a small, quaint moment I do not think, process, or reminisce, I just sit back on an old wooden lawn chair enjoying the velour taste of this man's weed. But I speak too soon, as a snare drum announcing the approaching army. I cannot sit still. I chug my first drink and instantly focus on the fire-pit. I rummage around to find any inkling of what was burned. The only thing I can see is a couple more pieces saying 'Struggle'... and... 'Chris'. With a shrug I toss the paper back in the charred remains and continue to suck the roach with ease. I hate that I am doing this, but, at the same time, I feel the rationalization already present and accounted for. My mind calms to a velvet softness.

The chair is not wood; it becomes cushion when I know it is not. I have to get up; and so I do, to the shed, without motive. I trump through his over-grown grass to the entrance and see the same, brand new padlock. I try to jiggle, slam, bam, and shove with no unintended damage: nothing. There has to be something explaining, lurking. My thirst cancels the interest in the shed.

My re-entry in the house spoils me with the awesome power of music; I sharpen my hearing even though I didn't want to originally. The liquor is in the main room and the main room is "In-A-Gadda-Da-Vida": I think, 'Don't think, just observe'.

Lay on stomach, watching floorboard, an ant walks with military conviction, a mirror, water beside a mirror, reflection upon reflection, time is slow, no chair, sit on floor, drums, guttural voice screaming, same furniture, take my hand, please take my hand- for what?, it makes no sense to sit on floor, walk to wall, speak to wall, pat it, we're friends now, drums thunder, cymbals break like crystals from 10 stories high... I have to move ... to the next room... this is high school bullshit. But I feel superior right now.

The newly-labeled living room, off the hallway, L-shaped, plays "Heroin": I enjoy walking into the end saying, "… I guess that I just don't know."

The song repeats- this old man knows how to set an experience. I listen.

> **"I don't know just where I'm going**
> **But I'm gonna try for the kingdom, if I can**
> **cause it makes me feel like I'm a man**
> **When I put a spike into my vein,"**

Floating is based on words, not fact. Collapse safely to floor and crawl to first piece of furniture: an ottoman, a round, mushroom-shaped, leather dressing.

Regain senses, see window with odd reflection. I stare and listen.

> **I have made the big decision**
> **I'm gonna try to nullify my life**
> **cause when the blood begins to flow**
> **When it shoots up the droppers neck**
> **When I'm closing in on death**
> **And you cant help me not, you guys**
> **And all you sweet girls with all your sweet silly talk**
> **You can all go take a walk**
> **And I guess that I just don't know**
> **And I guess that I just don't know**

Find a mirror, been there for years, on the floor, why? He must've been here, too. Smoke and drink are mixing well- I should get another, too tired, no, go get it, won't be long, too comfortable…too … soft, and fluffy… tempo… picks up- yes, I know, yes, I understand, why, right now…?

> **Where a man can not be free**
> **Of all of the evils of this town**

And of himself, and those around
Oh, and I guess that I just don't know
Oh, and I guess that I just don't know

I need to move, can't- wait, wait for the right time,

Because when the smack begins to flow
I really don't care anymore
About all the jim-jims in this town
And all the politicians makin crazy sounds
And everybody puttin everybody else down
And all the dead bodies piled up in mounds

The thoughts are bad, must walk out, get up, center myself, move on... but the remnants of the chorus linger,

And thank God that I just don't care
And I guess I just don't know
And I guess I just don't know

To the next room: a small enclave of a stairwell leading to the loft, where the trees sang, and the leaves... the leaves... dance, yeah. "The End"... I know this one. The repeat function is phenomenal... it just began as I walked in... because I find this is the day, the day my friend... or foe, you, TC, aging lil' mofo.

I don't look, I just sit, right... on the fucking floor. The voice begins,

Lost in a roman...wilderness of pain
And all the children are insane
All the children are insane
Waiting for the summer rain, yeah

I laugh in my 'droned' state... I listen and feel the fibers of the carpet reach into my cheek and make hooks, they want me too. I've never felt so wanted.

There's danger on the edge of town
Ride the kings highway, baby
Weird scenes inside the gold mine
Ride the highway west, baby

I feeble and wobble… laugh… the snake is … long… a creature no lest but to nurture only brings trouble… the car is moving – I feel powerless! I sit, I watch, I'm scared. Then a faceless man walked down the hallway….

He went into the room where his sister lived, and…then he
Paid a visit to his brother, and then he
He walked on down the hall, and
And he came to a door…and he looked inside
Father, yes son, I want to kill you
Mother…i want to…fuck you

I don't know what to say! I … I … am living! Let the mind go! – Shapes speak, colors talk back, carpet pushes back, walls are paranoid… I am by myself… I leave out necessity… the last lyrics I here-

C'mon Baby, take a chance with
Us, meet us at the blue bus… c'mon!

Then I hear a scream as I leave…what I am I doing…?

The last room is off the hallway. I run to the liquor and make two tall drinks, awaiting the Devil Incarnate to show based on my misfortunes and faults. Nothing shows amidst the incredible mixture of psychedelic rock… I move to the last room with out cheating… even though I am … wondering… if… this-

"Kashmir" by Led Zeppelin, it just began, I actually skip

into to the room like I was missing a premiere of some sorts. The Eastern philosophy in me falls right now, that joint was… tainted… dude can't get good weed… like this…

"But not a word I heard could I relate, the story was quite clear
Oh, oh.
Oh, I been flying… mama, there ain't no denyin
I've been flying, ain't no denyin, no denyin

Ooh, yeah-yeah, ooh, yeah-yeah, well I'm down, so down
Ooh, my baby, oooh, my baby, let me take you there

Let me take you there. let me take you there

I heard enough! I want answers. I go to the kitchen table as instructed. I am for one to always abide by the rules- too bad, not all can count.

The sheet in the drawer says:

'Grab the other joint and go in the bathroom. It's pretty much sound proof, Turn on the tub and smoke your joint. Light the candle and turn off the light. Strip down to your boxers and smoke out the joint. Now hit play on that little tape recorder and lay motionless in the water…. Just listen to a poem I call "Life's Suspended Dream." I wrote this when I was high, but recorded it later when I was sober'.

I am exhausted with his shenanigans but I fill a tub with bath water, draw it, prepare, and strip to my jeans, no socks…what else do I have to do?

I lie in the tub, push Play, and listen… the scratching sound of silence building is large, heightening:

Remain still... close your eyes

LET YOURSELF GO
TO ANOTHER PLACE IN TIME
ANOTHER FRAME OF MIND
WHERE YOU ARE UPSIDE DOWN
AND TURNED AROUND

MOTIONLESS
IN SPACE
LIKE THE EARTH
(SUSPENDED)
FEELING NOTHING
AT ALL
IN THIS WORLD
YOU FALL
WHERE NO ONE CAN CALL
FOR NO ONE
IS HERE AT ALL

[left speaker]
In still water
Paled faces
Reflections of
Unknown places

[right speaker]
Lights are flashing
People changing
Hear the words
They are saying

...what do you feel
...What do you see
...in life's suspended dream

You come to a hallway

You move very slowly
Towards someone
A friend – waiting
A doorway

Remain still… open your eyes
To the lit up sky
Revolving around you

And you can see

The world
From an overview
Where people laugh
In tangents
And others scream
In sorrow

   [left speaker]
   Earth is moving
   Colors fading
   View the picture
   The world is painting

…What do you feel
…What do you see
…In life's suspended dream

A time of life and horror
In god and space
A garden of ecstasy
In this unknown place

[seven seconds of complete silence]

   [left speaker]

Come back

[**right speaker**]
A voice is screaming

Is god dreaming
A voice is screaming

…what do you feel
…what do you see
…in life's suspended dream

You come out of a doorway
And onto a highway
With the past
Behind you
And a tunnel
In front of you
No one
Is beside you

[The sound of deep breathing – every few seconds]

The time is seizing
The doors are breathing

I can hear you
I can feel you
But I can't see you
I can sense you
Where are you
I could be you
Who are you
Who are you
Who are you?

The tape clicks; I shoot up as a refugee caught,

immediately feeling guilty. The room is dark. I am in my fucking jeans, soaked, no shoes or socks, no shirt, and I have to go home. No concept of time: a miraculous achievement.

A piece of paper glides on the porcelain tile as if the door tossed it to me, ending perfectly on my eyes:

SLEEP IN THE SPARE BEDROOM

I am water-logged, I am disturbed: I immediately follow his map and crash out of spite. How dare he make me ruin my best jeans... there should be women...

Ted Christopher walks in:

"What words do you remember? What can you recite back to me?"

I take the drink from his hand and see an intense pyre of fire behind his excited eyes. His energy is released. I rattle around inside my head for any tidbit to latch my memory onto. The seconds lumber by as I listen to a chop-shop, a marching band. He is going to notice my lack of attention.

"I cannot say I do, Ted Christopher. It does not mean that I do not understand. It simply means-"

"It simply means I may have made a mistake with you. I don't want to pace around this place and question my intuition. Maybe it wasn't for a reason. Maybe I just simply made a mistake."

"Wait a minute. You just can't simply throw your hands up and toss me to the side."

"YES, I can. Do you want to stay? Do you want to learn? Do you want to learn about love; learn about the simplicities of everyday life? Trust me, we all wear blinders, our faces stuck in the muck of now, now, NOW! My songs are spread out over various places that commemorate my journey and re-connect my past with my present. I have one simple question: Are you in or are you out?"

He opens his planner and scribbles a note, tears it out, and stuffs it into his robe pocket.

"Well, sure, but I can't just get up and leave work and other commitments."

"Yes you can."

The diamond shine of his tone cuts sharply into my glass house of apprehension. He is right: why not? This is not some run-of-the-mill procrastination or Peter-Pan romp. This may be a sojourn I need. He smiles with a radical discretion to what he reveals.

"Pack light, for the treasure is... for anyone."

He leaves; I fade to sleep pondering his last words.

CHAPTER 7

TO LEAVE A LIFE YOU KNOW BEHIND

With a snort, I suddenly awake! I am on a rug, a blanket, a what-the-fuck-scan. It has to be the spare bedroom; I don't know but it might be my own imagination. Exiting is a blinding, advanced exercise. I go to the stair-case. How did I get out of the tub? I step down in thought: clothes still damp, cold and tight, no socks, damn, I hate not wearing socks.

I reach the bottom of the stairs to sunlight assailing my blood-shot eyes. My head throbs with each quick chirp from a bird: I wish it was dead. The path I use when I arrive requires concentration… effort to arrive at the kitchen table, which I originally thought was a surgical slab, based on the purified interior decor.

This dull, gray brain of mine pounds for release from my lobe: I think that weed; that smoke, that grass, that pot, that Devil's cabbage, was laced. With what- it wasn't Windex, I can say that.

Ted Christopher sits at the table, so majestically and smug, drinking a beer. He looks up from the Sunday Plain Dealer.

"Well good morning, Pumpkin! Did you sleep well?"

I can barely function; I just grunt, instantly think what the fuck is a pumpkin: it's him. I fumble, bumble, stumble towards the fridge and hear him as if he was a drill sergeant in menopause.

"Orange juice on the top shelf…"

I pick up the orange juice.

"AND KEEP IT ON THE TOP SHELF, Vodka in the freezer."

I go for the vodka in the freezer, but before-

"-AND KEEP IT IN THE FREEZER, one shot will make you feel like a bull, two shots will make you feel like a missionary."

I grab a glass and make my stupid little drink.

"Don't forget to throw in a strawberry, or a blueberry, or whatever you young guns eat."

I think strawberries, I think blueberries, I even think bananas… but this charade is testing my hung-over patience: who the hell is this guy? I sit down and try to read the back side of his paper. I see an article saying that, "… for every drop creates a flower to believe…"

That's enough. I can't read from this distance in this state of mind. He creases the paper and sets it on the table and stares at me; he laughs. He knows what I'm going through: a constant barrage for recuperation or a selfishness of more sauce. My actions seem to outpace my thoughts by a mile; I close the vodka bottle.

"What are you staring at old man?"

He just shakes his head.

"Stupidity."

All of a sudden, he closes his eyes and takes a deep breath. His arms are in the air as if he is the savior of the world. He bellows.

"Fall."

I notice the window is open and I can feel the cool breeze. He continues with his eyes closed.

"It's the end of spring; the end of summer. The leaves outside are changing colors and beginning to fall from the trees. It is part of nature you know, the natural order of things. Nothing, my friend, remains the same. You learn what you live and die before you ask the question."

I listen with little conviction but pause subconsciously. He breathes in deeply.

"Life is not about God... well, scratch that. It's not about you. It's not about me. It's not about drugs. It's not about work or whatever you study in college. It's not about nature or what you see from a car window. It's not about a movie or what you hear on the radio. It's not about money or fame or a fast car and a mansion in Malibu. It's not about dreams. It's more than that."

He opens his eyes and stares at me with a tear in his eye.

"It's simple... the only thing that matters. Make yourself another drink and follow me outside to the deck."

His voice has a way of exploding.

"Beneath the rock on the table you will find a poem. Lie in my hammock and read. I wrote the poem when I was in high school. It was inspired by my high school sweetheart. God, she was beautiful. I could have probably written the poem when I was five. I don't know, but I am tired. I'm going upstairs and going to sleep. You know your way out."

He leaves. I can hear his heavy footsteps on the carpeted stairwell. I can't stop volleying 'Who is this man? Is he somebody famous? Where did he come from?' I am so messed up right now that I don't even know if he is a ghost. I do what he says out of sheer subservience. I make another drink and throw in a strawberry, a fruit fly flies from my glass. So I get a new one? I shrug and walk outside, lift the rock and grab the poem. I lie in his hammock, sip my fruit fly cocktail and read.

<u>LOVE</u>

Bluer than water in the sea
Greener than leaves found on a tree
It is in you and me
Yes, you and me - my love

We're more colorful than a picture in a magazine
Happier than an actor in an unrealistic scene
When the world is unclean

Love
Love

It's safer than a vehicle that can fly
Better than a *drug* that makes you high
Just give it a try, before it all will die

Love
Love

Bluer than a picture of the sky
Greener than the grass that lies…
…Beneath you and I
Yes, you and I – my love

We're more beautiful than *artwork* in a cathedral hall
Livelier than a mannequin in a *suburban* shopping mall
When the world is small

Love
Love

It's lighter than a man on the moon
But heavier than a playground on a Sunday afternoon
In an air balloon, I'll find you soon

Love
Love

It's sharper than a dagger
More lethal than a *knife*

And I'm higher than a kite
When I'm with you – my love.

I finish and leave myself to swing casually, back and forth, back and forth. The rhythm is soothing to my catatonic state of last night. From a window above, *Imagine* by John Lennon parades into his backyard for the trees and nature to participate. To Imagine, I try, but it hurts; I'd rather sip my drink and let the music just wash over me without an effort to actually catalog or interpret. It is nice: nice, you couldn't get a simpler statement than that. It is nice. To say something so plain yet so, so simple that you cannot read into it anymore than the 8 letters it signifies: it... is... nice. I laugh to myself since I have less than a day to decide on the madness that is being here at this old man's house, reading his old poetry, drinking his old liquor, and probably swinging on this old hammock. What a life.

I finally muscle the energy to get out of the hammock and fetch another drink. I quickly finish it and head to my car. Might as well go back to my place and think rationally with a twelve pack on the way to help make the pros-cons of this charade without an audience. I forgot I had his poem 'LOVE' in my pocket still. I toss it on the passenger seat and the last line that stands out is "... it's lighter than a man on the moon, ... but heavier than a playground on a Sunday afternoon..."

If there was such a feeling associated with love, than I misunderstood with my high school sweetheart.

†

A late autumn crux to a night, listening to Bush, "Mouth": my girlfriend of three years sitting passenger. We don't have to talk when I drive; we understand each other's thoughts, but mislead ourselves by this arrogance, presumably mine.

"Aren't we supposed to go to his place?"

"Yeah, I'm going there now."

"Okay."

The breeze just flows through the car… nothing more.

†

I sit in my place: it's turned into a cliché, rock star's hotel room: furniture over-turned, food on the floor, footprints of… whatever. I just realize that a mirror was broken. There was no reason for that mirror to be broken. It was totally off to the left of the hallway… fuck. Shit! It almost passes for a Motley Crue room minus the drugs, the drums, the drunks, the dames. Phone rings. It's my parents. The staccato nature of my responses is not dynamic at all: yeah… hello… I do… I know… I love you both… you guys good?… really?… she hasn't called… I know I should… who cares right?… anyway, tell dad I love 'em, bye.

I push play on the stereo and it shuffles to Metallica, "Wherever I May Roam". I sit back down and laugh. Really laugh. I get up and rush for my largest bag: an Air-Force bag from the Korean War given to me by my father. I load it up with two pairs of pants, two boxer-briefs, two button shirts, two white shirts, two pairs of socks, and walk to the stereo. The chorus is playing…

"… And the earth becomes my throne…"

Something's missing… I knock the home phone off the

61

receiver. Now it's an official rock star's hotel room.

✝

The breeze just flows through the car... nothing more.
    "You never said where- whose house?"
    "Does it matter?"
    "You don't have to be an asshole!"
    "I'm not being an asshole- you just get on my nerves."
    The silence grinded into me even though I didn't flinch; a stolen glance over to her and her face would slice me ever so finely. These slits add up. Until the blood loss is unchecked and it's time to let her go. She cried; I didn't. I wish I did- could have been healthier if the roles were reversed.

✝

I drive by that same intersection, alone, and think of the differences one little decision, one little theory can possess. The ripple-effect can change the past, this present, and our future. The song, 'Heaven Beside You' by Alice In Chains plays, stoking these embers. I loved my high-school sweet-heart, I did. It just never showed. I shake back to task at hand: a case of cold beer. The afternoon on a Sunday is always interesting, lively, and peculiar: the cashier is a guy that is not peculiar: the quick marts employ people who could have made a difference but opted out due to consistent uphill struggles. I scold myself for rudely pigeon-holing this order of people, then there's me who just bought a case of beer. As I reach closer to his house, the fading and closest memory of my high school sweetheart is lame and uncharacteristically void of the good times. The old man's memory of his sweetheart appears too grandiose that I question if it's remotely true.

The house is the same open canvas: few lights, ominous trees over-hanging. My car windows are down and I hear a distinct difference.... Is that Ozzy Osbourne playing...? Recent stuff too? Yes, it is. I close my eyes, take one last drag of my cig, flick into the street, grab my duffle bag, deep breath, open my eyes and head in. The resolution of the right choice illuminates bright within. The beer can wait.

CHAPTER 8

CAN AN ANSWER BE FOUND
IN THE CHAOTIC CONFUSION OF REALITY?

I cross the threshold as if there was an imaginary turn-stall to an amusement park: the place is crawling with hordes of people from all classes, coming to and fro in revolving cliques. The illumination of the right choice just faded to the right to be wrong. I waft through the menagerie and free-associate this and that with how and what. There's a bohemian clique off the main foyer playing hacky-sack and crashing into tables and the wall, leaving their distinct mark of lacking skills. I continue through the hallway and see another group, men and women, dressed in typical leather and chaps doing beer bongs, painting the carpet and walls with the end foam, each contestant adding more and more to the funnel. Their words I overhear are a mixture of nonsense, like:

"You ever chop wood?"

"I'm going to a festival..."

"You should see my last costume..."

"Ghost buffalos live! I swear...!"

One particular beer-bonging participant slinks by, grabs me for balance, offering his two-cents:

"I feel the language falls like rain or sleet, I laugh, naked I turn and find all the sudden stop is because the lines of the newspaper don't match. SO! I can, I will, I will win!"

I have to say I'm happier that it wasn't to puke even though he is naked. This circus is unbelievable. I go into the kitchen where the kitchen table has a garbage can of punch and fruit, with a 40 year old woman, one large breast in the bra, the other swinging freely, gathering the attention of all around her.

"I am still Iron Maiden. As the radio voice tells me I carry the child of David Lee Roth, it turns out to be a homo, a homo.... SAPIEN!"

I venture through a kaleidoscope of distraction, confusion, worry, and concern: mayhem is everywhere. A man with the best handle-bar mustache I haven't seen on TV walks by with aviator sunglasses, saran wrap and red body paint. I get cold-cocked by the smell of ketchup: why ketchup?! Another clique occupies the room where I first sat with Ted Christopher: the room was so structured and diagrammed; it's now a clan of men in the most stereo-typical pimp attire, I wonder: did they break into the wardrobe department at Playhouse Square? The ace of spades in the ribbon of one dude's hat is sweet; no doubt this can be a fad... again. I make it to the liquor cabinet after passing more people, who I have to admit are amazingly nice and obviously bizarre. They rant nonsense but I hear their meaning over the sound.

"Ba-dum-tah! The drum beats again!"

"A new beginning, brother. Kiss is the way, the sun, the steel, it shines."

I didn't think there would be any liquor: lo and behold, I am deliciously wrong. I hastily make a drink as my Air Force bag is tripping people. For some unknown mystery, their nonsense gels into my short-term memory:

"Ever seen tomatoes rot in the sun?"

"I ... have looked at the pantry... of my own life... and I keep going. Who doesn't want a second chance?"

What is it with Kiss' music: it's just the same thing... but, millions of fans can't be wrong? Get this girl with the patch over her eye:

"I love this guy, this guy right here, he is my Swiss-cheese, the holes, the fault of missing things... it is the next brain-on-drugs commercial."

I take my drink and my bag and head for the stairs: the host of this magnificent, albeit disturbing, carnival has to be somewhere. And with answers. Suddenly, I'm yanked out of the hallway, by a girl, at least: the youngest one so far.

"If I pour music into my head... it jingles with ice cubes, the drink hollows out the noise. Drink some!"

She tries to empty her head into my glass. I try not to shock her with the results.

"Thanks, babe, but you gave me some already."

"Oh, okay."

She skips away with a contentment rarely seen today. I finish my drink and I am compelled to make another one before going upstairs. I briskly achieve this small accomplishment and make it up the stairs, but not before I have to dodge a fruit fight, a group of three people chanting in the same monotone voice, and a pile of piano keys- where the hell was a piano?! Upon reaching the loft, a slight serenity is found but quickly shuddered away by the awaiting people outside the same door I saw Ted Christopher, TC, enter the previous night. For some reason, they eerily part and gesture me to open the door. If this turns out to be a religious fanatic I will be sorely upset at believing his words could be action. I knock on the door and enter. Three sophisticated women in business suits, Caucasian, Asian, and African-American, close their briefcases. The imperial skin of the trio is porcelain and godlike. TC clicks a pen and tosses it into the wall with the force to make it stick. The women pass by me.

"Good. I see you packed."

"What the hell is going on here?"

"Them? The lady friends are none of your concern; not all things are relevant, my friend. Come, we start the next chapter tonight. Oh! You didn't drink the punch from the garbage can did you?"

"No."

"Good, someone thought they would help everybody out by adding a sheet of LSD to it. Sad, but who am I to judge. I am not God."

He passes by me in a bath robe; I grab his arm.

"This is insane. What the hell is all this? I thought you said we were going somewhere."

"Perception is not always reality, kid."

"Why are all these people here?"

"Questions don't always need answers. I placed some flyers around, announcing my departure. Interesting taverns, interesting hideaways, interesting places turn up interesting people. Again, who am I to judge; in the end, it will make sense. I also needed some equipment on such short notice. Here, put these on."

I catch noise-reduction earphones. He leaves me behind in a quicksand of more questions: each one I ask gets me deeper, further from grasping the so-called big picture. Then I hear it. A jack-hammer is on somewhere in the house. I drop my bag in his room and run downstairs, and run downstairs again to the basement of the noise. A large throng of people circle around a hole in the concrete floor fight-club style; TC waves me over to him.

"Ready for your next song? Hit it Chump!"

An enormous bear of a man triggers the jack-hammer; I rush to put the head-phones on. The absolute noise coupled with the drinks, the scope of surrealism here is enough to make anyone swoon with over-stimuli. The noise stops; the circle cheers; a voice from the hole.

"I reached it!"

TC raises his arms in the air: the people gathered hinge on his words as if he was a messiah.

"Alright people! Pineapple upstairs and then wrestling in the backyard. Let's go."

And with a unanimous Viking yell, the circle unravels to the stairs and up.

"Your house? Everything in this house is destroyed you know?"

"Material things, it doesn't matter."

The bear in the hole raises a box to TC.

"Go over to that stereo, read this with only candlelight. A bottle of wine is uncorked."

I am compelled by TC's aura: I blink, I breathe, I comply.

"I left my job and place for this?"

No answer; he's already upstairs. It's just me, this metal box, a bottle of wine, and a stereo with 'Ode to Joy', Beethoven's 9th Symphony. I do as told: I open the box and read.

The Fraternity of Mankind

Our world... together
As if we were one
Our father... forever
Pray upon his only son -
His only son...

Help us

Understand the reasons why
We live here
Beneath your bright blue sky
In such a beautiful land
In such a beautiful time
Listening, to this-

Most beautiful band

Play the image
That is in your mind
Of a story
That brings you hope
And a time of glory
Of when you were young

And innocent

To the time
And to the place
Where you saw her crying-
Like years before
When his hands and feet
Were raised and torn
And blood flowed down
From a ring of thorn
The woman and children
Could only mourn
For today
It wouldn't matter if he was even born.

What have we become?
What we said
We would not have done
To our father, and his son
What have we become?

We drove them far from home
When we took their land away
Now they have to roam
When all they wanted was to stay
How do you feel, today?
I wonder

Why

Why couldn't he say good-bye?
To catch her in the rye
And where were you-
Did you cry?
The day, the day
An American hero -was left to die

And we can hear his music
And we can hear his words
So listen

Will we ever have?
Will we ever see?
Will we ever be?
A fraternity of mankind

Here on earth

In the Garden of Eden
We fight for our freedom
If it's what you believe in.
If it's what you believe in.
If it's what you believe in.

The older we are
The more we lose sight
And why can't we get it right
When history repeats itself
The more lethal we fight

In the night

Satellites
Are a spying device
And Gods word
Is no longer advice.

Science has become a journey
Where a natural alloy is a flying machine
And an assembly line, a future being
Night vision -what's that you're seeing

Sadness
And
Pain?

Barricades
Or
Hope?

Will these words
Create music
In this soul?

It's to Tennyson
It's to Frost
And it's to all
That has been lost
For the words
That had no cost
I thank you
It's a generation
You hoped to save
In the roads
You paved

Under heaven

A life
And a liberty
A declaration
And a freedom
To be independent

And sign
A fraternity of mankind

And the sand slipped through our hands.
And the music blared his last stand–

The 4'Th movement...

The Roman Empire succeeded to a civilization in Greece.
Where pyramids in the desert map out the stars in space.
It's a correlation in relation, to our destination.
This relaxation is a sensation, but not a recreation

Just listen

From America and terror
To Iraq and Iran
From L.A and a dream
To a president turned king

It's a democracy

All pawns
In isolation
Serving
Under segregation
In search of
Solutions
Full of
Pollution.

Will we ever have–
Will ever be–
A fraternity of mankind?

The blacks
And the jews

Cannot belong.
While the rich
And the poor
Pretend to be strong.

The muslims
And the whites
Wait too long
While the living
And the dead
Sing this song...

Will we ever see poetry?
In the signs and the places.
Will we ever hear music?
In the trees and different races.

The older we are
The more we lose sight
Why can't we get it right
When history repeats itself
The more lethal we fight

In the night

She wrote: People are really good at heart.
He thought: Leading a country made him so smart.

When he never even looked
At the information in the book
And we call Nixon the crook.

Will we ever have-
Will we ever see-
Will we ever be-
A fraternity of mankind?

Here on earth
Under heaven
In this lifetime
I have seen-

Tragedy
Within our nations
And victims
In our streets
Where food
Is no longer there for the weak
And farmers
Are unable to grow their wheat.

What have we become?
What has this world done-
To our father and our son?
We are put on this earth
To become one
To become one
To become one

And I can hear it
It's playing
Off in the distance -I hear it
The music is playing
And it's loud
So listen
To what I am saying:

In the back of a room
At a table of grace
It comes in color
But leaves no trace
Upon the time
He reveals his face
Once again

Here among us
Once again
In this beautiful land
In this beautiful time
If it's in your mind
We can find
And we can find
A fraternity of mankind

I sit paralyzed in the candlelight from emotions which cannot be broken down into smaller parts. The seedlings of reason into the sight of the future are sown. Suddenly, TC runs down.

"Get your shit; these people have taken this party to another level."

I don't hesitate. A houseful of people on LSD: what could they be doing?

I see what he means. "Killing in the Name of" by Rage Against the Machine has infiltrated the entire environment, every seam of air. Fires are evolving everywhere in his house. I lose TC. I begin to run out the back-door, and then I remember my bag. I go after it but the flames are growling everywhere upstairs, I run back down. The smoke, to coughing, to being buzzed, my parents worrying, high school sweetheart crying, the police – I'm tackled!

TC helps me up and rushes out the backdoor; I follow.

"You're a dumbass! I said go outside."

"You're the asshole. I saw you running back into the house."

"For these!"

He holds up a pile of singed letters, postcards, and sealed envelopes.

"Follow me, I have a different car on the other side of the woods."

Harleys begin circling the fire as if it was a Rolling

Stones concert. I look forward and just follow TC into the woods. The scene behind was unreal: the fire was singing along with all the people outside rooting for it like an audience with TC being the announcer.

"Come on, it's just a house. It is just... a house."

CHAPTER 9

CAN REGRETS AND CONSEQUENCES LEAD TO HOPE AND SALVATION?

Running through the dark woods, following a colored robe, I'm able to scourge some internal humor in the Catholic analogies, except for the LSD punch, the house on fire, and-

THUNK!

I hit the soiled earthen floor, floored. TC comes back and yanks me up.

"C'mon pumpkin. Watch out for those trees. They'll jump in front of you."

We make it to an idling Lincoln. I attempt a reasonable entry into a cabin of loud noise but get tossed into the leather seats.

"This ain't casual time! Hit it, Monyak!"

The music is muted; car accelerates, swerves, swerves again, full turnaround, accelerates- I've lost all direction since I've been rolling around as a marble on the back-seat floor. Gaining my composure and proper seat, a console is pulled down between me and him; an opaque box in the dark disguised the inventory of top shelf liquors. He makes two drinks, with ice. The mini-postcards lining the perimeter track lighting distracts me: San Jose, Monterey, Venice, Santa Monica, Malibu, New Orleans, Vegas, Chicago, New York City, and Denver, Colorado. A flash burns under my flesh.

"My car! My stuff!"

"Take this and relax. It's all just stuff."

"Like your house? I'm not as cool as you with losing possessions. Like my car!"

I grab the drink and place the cold glass against an oncoming knot from running into a tree.

"Read this."

"Not reading shit until you tell me what the hell is going on!"

He sits frozen with envelope extended, face blank: this situation irritates like poison ivy on my ass. I snatch it and read.

SMART BAR

The walls are caving in
The door is slamming shut
The voice in my head
Is screaming

The lights are flickering
The stairs are moving
The voice in my head
Is screaming

Everything... Is out of control

A black light
A mirror
On the ceiling

A gate
An elevator
Arrival

Girls
Dancing
Girls

Suspended
A cage

Foam

Everything... Is out of control

Lights
Every color
In my eyes

Techno
Ultra violence
In my ears

Drugs
Of every kind
In my mind
Everything... Is out of control

Cops
The National Guard
The entire Government

Outside

What do I do?
(Can't think)
Where do I go?

The bar empties
The street
In chaos

American freedom
Fights
American freedom

I watch
From the rooftop
I watch
And understand the reason

My life
Is significant

I stare
At the stars

I stare
At the stars

The read is sloppy and disjointed, the gaps cemented with frenzied concern of when this episode, this ride, this journey will devour me. I feel underpinned with guilt in leaving so suddenly, and I am not being presumptuous in predicting a waste of debauchery and dismantling of ambition: a sub-chapter that writes itself has no need for advice; it materializes and fills the void of success so eloquently. But you also need luck to be elastic and forgiving. I re-read the poem. His veiled, random spurts of grandiose thoughts that keep the drug known as emotions running rapid prevents me from falling asleep.

TC stares out the window into the faint rain collecting on the window. His countenance speaks volumes without a flicker of emotion. It's as if this scenario has played itself out before, as the symphony of his life is reaching another opus with myself as the fledgling first-chair soloist, nervous and sweating with anticipation of how it will sound or if it will fly through the acoustically balanced walls of the recital hall.

I don't bother to look outside since I can tell we are on some back-roads, maybe an interstate, probably on cruise control: a precipice that we are on our way for at least an hour or two somewhere in this car. I find the quickest thought to be so easily answered with the faintest effort: have a drink, might as well right? So I let my resolutions make a mockery of the transpired events in some rationalizing 'could-be-worse' equations. The thought process falls like a sediment, as my tide of curiosity ebbs and flows until a visible shoreline of tremendous hypotheticals surface. What if I was as significant as I imagine? I would find it easier to quit drinking than probably exit this car and call the entire escapade off.

I continuously argue with myself incomprehensibly. Motionless in the car and the ample freedom to do and say whatever attracts the first symptoms to madness: a title I so often attribute my life around. But the indispensable fact is impulsively leaving without legitimate contemplation. To calm the quickening shouts of my parents' or peers' universal statement, 'What are you, stupid?' is weak and feeble at best. We could ask a hundred people to have a mass conversation about this matter and it would nevertheless turn into a series of rants, raves, and slogans, simply forgotten once the hundred people left the hall. So why bother? I grab another drink.

"You are quiet."

The first words out of TC: no change in speed or direction.

"What is there to say? Obviously I jumped into this rabbit hole you prepared so deviously, and now, I am at your side despite my instincts."

A snort.

"I can easily let you go back to your meandering ways of mediocrity."

I smirk at his smugness: nothing wrong with confidence.

"However... I do find this to be funny. This windfall of

you gas-bagging, 'it will make sense later' could be in my favor. Who says you can't find a reason amidst nonsense and chaos? I'll stick around."

With a nod, he goes back to his stare out the window. I was so close to pry, to delve into his past, such as: ever been married, currently on the prowl with an online dating service, hell, maybe he has a stash of mistresses, bank accounts across the globe. I notice the track of thought to be so trashy and worthless. Would that information shine any light upon this? I actually answer myself and say no. I lean back and let the tonics slow my mind to a meditative state wondering where the treasure is. The last thing I hear is a distant voice, 'you have to remember the past before you let go of the past.'

Debussy 'Suite bergamasque –
3. clair de lune' plays.

Half asleep, I look up and see him wipe a tear from his eye.

"You all right?"

"I'm fine, just looking at the moon. Someday, you'll understand."

I shrug his response off; listening is not the same as hearing. I peer out the window to witness darkness playing an antagonistic role with the headlights, navigating through the country hills and fields, until a sign 'Valley City' passes by. The Lincoln suddenly slows down, jerking me from half-asleep to full awakening. A large stone statue of Jesus spreading his arms creeps by my window. At this time of night, the marble is magnificent; the pose is commanding: it's something Italy flaunts everyday. The divider comes down from his trigger on the console.

"Turn left here, follow the winding road and park by

number 11."

I have so many simmering questions: where are we, why are we in a cemetery? Is it his mother, his father, his high school sweetheart? What, why, who? So many questions in my head, it sounds like a scratching record.

The trunk pops free and he gets out of the car. Should I get out or stay where I am. The curiosity is plausible since he grabs a sleeping bag from the trunk and walks towards a tombstone. He yells without looking back.

"Come on!"

I get out of the car with released haste and follow. I lose him for a brief moment only to walk around a tree and see him sitting Indian style. I sit down beside him, not Indian style; I'm prepped to listen, not to hear.

"This is my childhood friend and college roommate. We were freshman, had no idea what was to come. We were on the verge of becoming adults. I was stupid, experimenting with drugs. He was genuine. He never even drank and loved children. He was a good kid. He went home on a Saturday morning to referee a kids' basketball game at Brunswick Rec Center. He ran back and forth and blew the whistle. I guess he got light headed, I guess there was a foul. My lifelong friend and college roommate fell over and hit his head on the bleachers. He died instantly. His mother called that day. The phone rang. I finally answered. She said: 'Teddy, why is my son dead? Why is my son dead? Teddy, why is Kenny dead?' I had no answer."

He looks over at me; he expressively shakes his head, shouting.

"Billy Joel said it best: only the good die young. People like me have to figure out their purpose to get into heaven. The moment he died was the moment I began to live. One Life! Get comfortable, kid. There is a blanket in the backseat if you need it. I'm sleeping out here."

I opt for the Lincoln and relax into it. The driver: I can't tell if he is there or not. He probably has some pilgrimage, too. I make a small drink and let the leather envelop me. I drift off. But not before I realize inside my vast expense of consciousness how fragile life is. And it leads me to think of my mortality, my awareness of absolute truth that I cannot and will not avoid death. A tear streams down my cheek. Please go to sleep. Please turn off, Mind.

CHAPTER **10**

IS IT JUST ANOTHER DAY?

I walk amongst lockers and on industrial block tile; I notice the cheap basic pattern. I turn around from the slightest tension of being followed. I am. Three teenage boys are slowly watching and taunting. I can't hear what they are saying but the intensity of their indistinguishable words push me to keep walking... walking through the school doors and onto a city street. I am discerningly older, taller; no one is behind me except storefronts. The sidewalk is roped off with the cheapest of tape. Anyone could easily walk underneath or even tear it. The crowds of average men and women, with average kids, looking down the street with no specific behavior to arouse them, to indicate their motivation; the vacuum of silence is eerie. I ask somebody a question but my words are quickly swallowed by this absence. I move rapidly away from the crowd to a Pontiac Grand AM and start the ignition. The alcohol sweat and shakes are intense, smoldering, pushing myself farther and farther away from the pedals. I'm driving the car from the backseat with no way to reach the brake. I panic; the roads. Are wet; it's dark. With streetlamps, I can't stop! I can't! Fucking stop!

Awake! A sprinkler has been dousing the left side of the car. A lawn mower can be heard. I look around and around again, for the umpteenth time, the sheer minutia of if I am alive or not explode past the threshold of consciousness rendering me vulnerable to my subconscious remnants. My dreams are gaining textual strength, perfectly stimulating my justified anticipations and fears. My cell phone reads 11.23am. I peer out the dripping wet window and, in between sprinkler splashes, I see TC making the sign of the cross... water splash... TC touching the tombstone... water splash... TC walking to the car with the sleeping bag rolled up, placing it back in the trunk. He enters the car jubilantly; I don't smile- he does.

"Good Morning, Pumpkin."

I don't move either but to nonchalantly shift over. I'm half hung over, half confused and just hungry. The ceaseless, senseless drinking carries baggage as lazy fog and irresponsible consequences. He rolls down the window, taps on the roof. Suddenly, "Where the Streets Have No Name," by U2, blares from the speakers. The Lincoln takes a left onto 303 and rockets to a gratuitous, illegal rate. Before I can respond to anything we jump train tracks, barreling in mid-air, and fly through the country.

"One Life!"

He screams; I hold on; a sign appears. Welcome to Brunswick: a city that continuously attempts to shake the pigeon-holed association of hillbillies and meatheads by adding street lights, fast food restaurants, and a ton of car dealer ships with the affinity of being proud and just in their swagger. But that's what I hear from the Strongsvillians. The Lincoln weaves in and out of the traffic like it's the Indy 500. Amazed amongst the confusion, I get a phone call and notice it's a creditor trying to find me. The rush of danger-seeking dissipates quickly and I smile. That's right: one life. And I should be at work right now- HA! I begin to laugh; he follows along too.

"Are we going to your childhood doing seventy?"

The radio miraculously increases higher; the Lincoln bananas into a high school parking lot. Brunswick High

86

School: I am always awed in its size and scope. At first glance you would assume it was a factory of some sort, seeing it about a mile long, constructed in a one floor style, ferocious in its strength of white brick. The graduating class always made the paper with its breath-taking number of six-hundred plus. My high school in Parma pales in comparison but I find the substance within my high school walls to be of… what the hell am I thinking of? I shake back to the ridiculousness of my current condition, placement, and the foreboding reason to be much more entertaining. I hone back to the U2 song. The Lincoln takes the black top road around the building.

I see teenagers in football practice, wind sprints to be exact; I see the full band marching: the tuba players, the drummers, the baton twirlers and trumpet players wandering the vacant part of the field. The Lincoln creeps down the road. I see a stadium with lights and banners. The car drives across a stony lot and parks by the athletes' only entrance. He gestures in his console as a proud captain; the song "Where the Streets Have No Name" begins again ever so loud.

"We shouldn't be here; we're going to get caught!"

"Who cares? You have to see this!"

He exits the car and I follow as his foolish assistant for the time being. The music is so loud. He grabs onto the fence and stares at the field. I inquisitively stand behind, patiently waiting for some bold, outrageous war cry.

"Everything led me to that moment. The stands were packed. The kids had their faces painted. I was playing football with my childhood friends. It was our moment in time. The stage was set. The opportunity and the childhood dream were seconds away… seconds away."

He points at the car.

"This song I played over and over in the shower before the game. I would hear this song in my head as I would run and I would run, holding the ball tight to my chest, dodging players, just trying to score the winning touchdown."

The song ends. He turns around and shakes his head in defeat.

"It doesn't matter."

He walks back to the car with his head down and gets in the car. What a strange reaction from this eclectic, often aggressive, individual. I briefly startle myself thinking I might have made some gross error. He might be having some breakdown and I'm the only person here, to hear his ramblings, his obligatory visit to his past. I, now, have to shake my head but enter the car with my head held high. We drive away, get back on 303 and enter a Burger King drive-thru. What kind of fucking haute cuisine is this? He casually orders four burgers, from the back seat; I reach into my back pocket.

"Keep your money. This entire trip is on me."

"Good, because damned if I'm gonna spend the last of my money on... double cheeseburgers."

He laughs; I don't.

"Money, it's the downfall of every great nation. When will society realize the importance of life?"

He pays and grabs the burgers. He starts to scarf down the food; he gestures for me to grab one. Although hungry, I pass. I point to the liquor and make myself a drink against the antagonisms of my empty stomach. The car heads north on Pearl Road.

"Why do you think you are here?"

"To be honest, I'm not sure. I ask myself every minute that and keep grabbing drinks because at least the booze is free- and... I guess the wonderful nourishment is too."

He laughs at my sarcasm.

"That's the whole idea. Your first impulse should make you wonder. One day you will figure it out."

"I can smugly lean back and go on this field trip around places I have been to and seen at least a hundred times... but this vagueness is wearing thin. C'mon, seriously. I admit your house being burned down and that... party...was truly an invitation combo to madness- but fuck it. Really."

"You know what; you're not so bad, kid. I understand your attitude. To be honest, it is what I expected. Just keep your distance from power, control and thinking and you'll be fine."

I stare out the window in a rolling boil.

"Besides, shouldn't you be at work right now?"

The drive is quick to St. Ambrose, a large brick and glass building of a Catholic church, well known for the clout of special events and speakers it attracts. I didn't query the significance since I was melancholy from the previous jaunt. I shake my head and hang it low... for no credible reason.

"No song to blare?"

He smiles politely. The parking lot is empty. The car stops in front. He exits the car and enters the church. I sigh, rubbing my eyes and repeat in a crescendo 'where am I going'. I succumb and exit the car with a genuine, break-the-car-door slam. I enter the church's nave with a complimentary whole-body breath of cool air. A cascade of calm flows over me unexpectedly, but albeit, welcoming. I locate TC kneeling before the altar. I walk down the center aisle and take notice to the wooden crucifix hanging from the ceiling. The stained glass windows and statue of Mary remind me of many years of upbringing, schooling, attending the Catholic Church with a dour mood. Since then, I have grown, no, evolved in a new age, enriched with a new appreciation to the context and the surroundings. I approach to his vocal boom.

"I was honored to have the opportunity to play Jesus on this very stage. I died on the cross and rose again. It was a school play, one that I will never forget."

He bows his head. My previous mood has now flipped back to the addictive Curious... again. He continues in lecturing melancholy.

"Find the bathroom and enter the furthest stall. Stand on the toilet seat and lift up the ceiling panel. You will find something I wrote a long, long time ago. Just sit and ponder the words."

His head stays bowed. I listen, I don't know why, but I listen, and exit the main area to find the men's room. I enter the only stall and slide the lock behind me. I figure privacy in a church bathroom is the most private I'll get so, no need to press my incredible luck. I stand on the toilet seat and remove the ceiling panel. I find a piece of notebook paper sending vindication to my incredulous mind. I close the ceiling and sit on the toilet seat. I chuckle inside, close the lid on the toilet and read:

IS THERE A GOD

Silently I awoke
Into a dream
Only to see
Destruction
On t.v

-la dolce vita

A child whispers
The leaves have fallen
A man wonders
Why the trees are bare
Into the night

I still stare
Like a child
I feel his fear

Coming over me
Surrounding me
It is all around me

Like darkness
That overshadows the light
These visions
Appear in my sight
They reappear, but disappear
Without warning
I see him there

Following orders
Obeying the law
Misunderstanding
The truth of it all

(When the leaves will fall)
I whisper…

Is there a god
Watching over one tonight
Showing one the light
Is there a god

A mother will bear the pain of a child
And a child will seek comfort from a stranger
When a stranger is someone you know in danger

Is there a god

{solo thoughts}
Upon my shirt I wear his stains

I try to wash them away
But the blood remains
Do you feel the same
Is there a god

When faith becomes obscure
And hope is as painful as fear
Where love-love is that reflection you see in the mirror
No one seems to care

(Why are the trees still bare)
I wonder...

Is there a god

To take this pain away
To do what the bible will say
To pray upon today

Is there a god

To show me the way
To give me a sign

Like water turning to wine
Now is the time

I exit the stall and look at myself in the mirror. I throw cold water on my face and neck. The blistering question that has precipitously followed like a shadow at high noon only to disappear when the sun goes down is TC's repetition 'It will make sense'. I feel flustered for I have not been able to categorize him except for outrageous. I remember... I remember a lesson from the Dominican priest, A.G. Sertillanges, a person who concentrated on the moral theories from St. Thomas Aquinas into his non-specialist work, *The Intellectual Life.* It was of an easy read, being a structural guide on progression with life agenda to one of scholarly and piety. His teachings were of simple humility, a way to let the outside noises fall off and not question one's existence. For the pursuit in what you love and the preservation within the few hours of anyone's busy hectic life should, and can be spent, reduce the dense matters for entrance of enlightenment and liberation to the soul... the solitude of one, he politely stated, was of Solitude, a capital S. The distractions in concerns were irrelevant to the divine pursuit. In order for this preservation, progress, Solitude was important to listen to the greatest songs on earth: nature at night. From the nightingale and the crickets, to the wind and unknown clatter, the scatter from all around must be delved into since the emptiness is of the utmost plenitude. Ultimately, when one has structured oneself into this practice, questions of 'Is there a God' will scatter and blow away with the wind. I gathered his teachings that said all will achieve this Divinity of God but I remember I missed that final class because of a night not spent in Solitude but in the company of a woman at a local tavern. Her name escapes me but I remember this lesson from years back. I lean back against the counter in puzzlement of how rapid and flowing words of such magnitude and impact come to me in my cluttered condition. I remember where I am. I wash my face again, clean up the water mess and appreciate the brief fluidity of those words.

I walk back, into the church, to find TC dipping a crucifix, locking eyes with me, in Holy Water from the middle section. I watch from the back of the church for safety. He clasps the necklace around his neck and walks to the front of the altar, surreptitiously numbering. I flinch nervously in case there is someone here I might know.

His pause begins with a walk down the steps from the altar stairs to the main aisle of the nave; he counts. After twenty-three steps, he turns to his right and sits down in the exact pew I was in; he turns towards me.

"Come, there is a God. Pray with me."

I blankly do not rebut but sheepishly look around. No reason arrives; I kneel next to him and fold my hands in prayer. He begins:

The Lord's Prayer

Our Father, who art in heaven,
hallowed be thy name.
Thy Kingdom come,
thy will be done,
on earth as it is in heaven
Give us this day our daily bread.
And forgive us our trespasses,
as we forgive those who trespass against us.
And lead us not into temptation,
but deliver us from evil.
For thine is the kingdom,
the power and the glory,
for ever and ever.

Amen

He and I make the sign of the cross. He exits bluntly. Something catches my eye where he just was: a small, almost illegible "tc" is on the seat. He shakes me out of my gaze.

"The only way to find your purpose is to revisit your past. Every person born into this world was born at a specific time and a specific place. This is not by accident. Everything happens for a reason."

CHAPTER 11

TO BE YOUNG AGAIN, LYING BENEATH THE STARS AND DREAMING.

We exit the church in single-file, jumping into the Lincoln. We turn on Pearl Road and head north. The ride is in silence. I feel content with the visit as I know he does. I react when I see Top of the Hill Tavern, thinking a pit stop might hit the spot, but the car takes a right onto Magnolia Drive, a suburban middle-class society of homes. The sun begins to set; the moon is faint but visible. I see the designer brick sign in a manicured lawn: Memorial Elementary School. The car enters and drives around the one story brick building. I see a huge playground with soccer nets and swing sets. The simpler days when sunset was the timer for all children playing to head back home. I smile to myself. I guess I could call work later tonight and tell them I was sick with explosive diarrhea.

All these visits are starting to disappoint though. I thought we were going on some wild, Las Vegas trip: him with the funds; me, drinking and gambling for him. He interrupts my daydream.

"Fifth and sixth grade: what fun. My friends and I were the kings of the school. Girls used to chase us around this playground. We would play tackle football on that soccer field. I was always the quarterback. I would choose my team; my best friends and we would battle through the rain and mud. No whistle could ever end the play. We would come back to class caked in mud and sometimes blood."

The Lincoln stops; he points at a playground, woodchips mark off the area. I see a swing set with six swings, monkey bars and a huge slide.

"I used to come here alone at night and swing, just swing. I always wanted to jump and see if I could snag a star, but for some cowardly reason, I would just hold tight to the chains. I guess it doesn't matter now."

His words sometimes irk me: I guess it doesn't matter now. Has to be one of his favorites; obviously it does matter or he wouldn't say it, but a hot flash of horror washes over me, bringing my head to my knees: my car. Fuck, it's outside his burnt house. Nice one.

"This car thing is killing me-"

He grabs a flashlight from his console, exits and pops the trunk.

"It's just a car, have a drink, loosen up- you only have one life."

He makes two shots and pushes one into my hand. He raises and shoots; I follow and then exit the car. I am floored by this exact moment of shaken poise. He grabs his sleeping bag from the trunk and throws me a blanket. I follow him through a field to a base of a hill. He lays down his sleeping bag and sits down with his arms around his knees. I lay down the blanket and sit down next to him.

"1020 Westchester. This is where I grew up. It's where my parents decided to live."

He shines the flashlight.

"See that plum tree? I would throw the football towards it- just to watch my friends jump in the air and land in the tree."

He shines the light elsewhere.

"See that maple tree? That tree scared the shit out of me. It would thunder and rain and all I could think about was the movie 'Poltergeist'. Late at night, when my parents were fast asleep, I would open that window and jump into the leaves. I would run to the top of the hill, pretty much where we are right now, and lie down and stare at the stars. Some nights I would fall asleep and wake up to the rising sun. I was a kid. I thought any dream was possible. Life never turns out the way you expect. It just doesn't... happen that way."

He puts his head in his hands. I expect to see a crying old man relive his epiphany when I have my car outside his stupid burnt home. I muster all the strength to be sincere with-

"Are you alright?"

He looks up.

"No."

I sit swaying with anxiety. He begins to orate with majestic precision,

TO THE VIRGINS, TO MAKE MUCH OF TIME.
A POEM BY ROBERT HERRICK

GATHER ye rosebuds while ye may,
　　Old time is still a-flying :
And this same flower that smiles to-day
　　To-morrow will be dying.

The glorious lamp of heaven, the sun,
　　The higher he's a-getting,
The sooner will his race be run,
　　And nearer he's to setting.

That age is best which is the first,
　　When youth and blood are warmer ;
But being spent, the worse, and worst
　　Times still succeed the former.

Then be not coy, but use your time,

> **And while ye may go marry :**
> **For having lost but once your prime**
>   **You may for ever tarry.**

He finishes as if he just finished a marathon. He points to a bedroom window far away.

"My high school sweetheart and I had a moment that no gods could ever take away. It was our first time. 'With or Without You,' by U2 was being played on repeat. She was young, five foot one about ninety-five pounds. She had silky dark hair and the biggest brown eyes you have ever seen. She was the definition of innocence. She was hope. I felt lost inside her. Her hair surrounded me and all I could see were her eyes. It was our world, a world that no one could ever have or ever reach. It was– it was the best moment of my life."

He stops to shake his head; I find myself actually listening and not caring about outside this moment.

"We were like Adam and Eve, naked, but so comfortable. She was my soul mate."

He lies down and stares at the stars. I stare at the window and actually picture her and him. It's a love story that most likely ended in sorrow due to growing in age. Why else for all the self-brooding and revisiting?

"I'm going to sleep. Tomorrow, when you wake up check the chimney, I'm not sure if it was water damage, erosion or just the foundation. It separated from the house and has been that way for twenty-three years. Bottom line, your hand will fit and you will find the first poem I ever wrote. I will be in the woods."

"That's it? Another night of–"

"Calm down. I would like to know if you are worthy. But it's too early to make that judgment. I see how eager you are but not everything you wish for in life can be done in one night. Good night."

I get up and walk back to the car. I actually see movement in the driver's seat. I approach, knock on the window. The music gets louder and a hand-gesture wave. It talks.

"Just listen. Sit in the back and have some drinks. Can't say anything more."

I tried to visualize the voice to a person but gave up and went into the backseat. I plop into the backseat and look around with the attention span of a fly. No magazines, no newspaper, nothing. I fix a drink with some kick and attempt to open the console. I can't open the console so I sit and listen to the song: 'Nightswimming' by R.E.M. The lyrics fit to Michael Stipe's voice as if some symbiotic contract was hammered out before he agreed to sing. I attempt the last stanza out-loud.

"... the photograph reflects, every streetlight a reminder, nightswimming deserves a quiet night..."

The tone-deaf approach butchers the meaning. I envy singers. The song ends and I look at the house, sizing up the chimney. I begin to rationalize what he said about reaching into the chimney, a chimney that no doubt, belongs to somebody else. This is a puzzle. He wants me to do it in the morning when the neighborhood is up and someone will see me and that will be that. I'll be brought up on whatever charges and then, then I will be interrogated about the fire at his house since my car was probably the only one left there. I roll my eyes.

"The shit that follows me."

I finish the drink and slam it down with conviction.

"Fuck it."

I exit the car and casually get to the sidewalk a couple of houses away. I walk the sidewalk and laugh to myself. I could never do this for a living. What living? My distraction in thought leads me to walk past the house. The word shit is repeated fourteen times. I get so agitated from this whole GD mess. I jog between the houses and stand by the chimney, tying my shoe. I frantically look around to any possible crevice, hole, loose brick. I can't believe I'm still tying my shoe. I thrust my hand around as if the sky was collapsing on me. Suddenly, I pass over a hand-sized gap, put my hand in expecting it to be bitten off by some ravenous animal, lose my hand to rabies and get arrested. I feel something plastic: I yank and pull out a zip lock bag and I jog away as if a stick is stuck up my ass. 'This is stupid' rains in my head. I make it back to the car and jump in. Out of breath, I slouch. I bet I don't get up from this position all night. But I have no drink to read this... I worm around the backseat and fix a drink.

Okay – all set. I start to ask myself if I'm drunk... and... do I need one?

"Dumbass, no fucking light."

I don't even contemplate walking back to TC for the flashlight: I'm not getting out of this car. I open the car door a little until it's completely wide open. No light. I lay back down on the backseat with a drink, a plastic bag, and no fucking clue of what this is. I sigh. I feebly crane my head up so the drink doesn't spill over the only set of clothes I have until... whenever. I sit in silence, in ignorance, in a gin haze, and begin to just simply... listen: no crickets or nightingales in the suburbs, just silence.

The next morning I wake up with the worst pain in three areas. My pants are wet, I touch my crotch and surrounding area: spilled the drink? I am relieved to conclude it was a spilled drink. I exit the car and find he is gone: to the woods, huh? I notice the closest woods to his child home and venture that way. I take a glance at the plastic bag and see notebook paper. I walk in and follow the only feasible path and reach a stream.

"Did you read it?"

I spin around, almost shitting my pants. He sits against a tree, chewing tobacco, staring into the stream.

"No! I got it last night since the morning would have been the worst time. Can't just go up to a house in the morning and start molesting their chimney."

"Well you're not like me. You don't have guts."

I drop my arms without even an ounce of argument in me.

"Relax, sit over there and just read."

"Just that simple. I fucking slept in the worst position-"

"Didn't have to. Had a blanket for you."

He spits into the stream.

"See the stream? See how the water flows?"

I glance over with no care to see a chunk of tobacco float. I watch the ripples and feel the mindfuck I am in.

"Never give up, kid."

He gets up, stretches and confidently walks away. I walk out of the woods, holding the plastic bag. He closes the trunk and looks at me with a shitty grin on his face.

"Every great writer has a masterpiece. The media and critics may be too stupid to ever understand."

I look at him; he just stares at the ground.

"My masterpiece began in North Royalton. Do you want to continue this trip or do you want go home?"

A minute goes by with an almost tangible ebb and flow of diplomacy and imagination from my body swaying.

"You know what? Yes! Yes I do."

I toss the plastic bag back at him. He doesn't even attempt to grab it.

"This has to be the undeniable, stupidest field trip that even a fourth grader would avoid. I mean, c'mon, visiting your high school, the church, although church was- the cemetery! Really? A cemetery! I know all this is relevant, epic for you and I get that. But for me to disrupt my life, lose my car, and my job to witness what? Your life. If I want to be a part of nostalgia I would watch PBS at home beating off with a cheesegrater. I mean, I ... I..."

I run out of words; his stare hasn't changed nor has his shitty grin.

"Fair enough."

TC gets in the Lincoln, rolls down the window. I try the car door but it is locked.

"Well, pumpkin. I tried to instill some wisdom, even some respect to what life is, but obviously, I was a fool. Oh well, oh well. If you're smart, you'll think about a girl."

The Lincoln peels off, a faint song of U2 is heard:

I want to trip inside your head
Spend the day there
To hear the things you haven't said
And see what you might see
I want to hear you when you call
Do you feel anything at all

I try to pin the title but I am hit with reality: I'm standing in the street of this Brunswick development, no car, no job probably, little money and a flashing battery on my cell. I guess it is fitting with all other things that have happened. I walk as calm as I can to the curb and squat. Big sigh. My eyes fixate on everything and nothing, then fall on the plastic bag...

I get up, pick it up and head back to the curb. A random car slowly drives by with the longest rubber-neck staring at me. Yes, I am a person sitting on a curb in the morning, afternoon, whatever.

Fucking people. I take out the piece of paper and read.

EARTH AND SKY

In the flowers and in the trees
The brightness of the leaves
In the land and in the sea
The earth and the sky
Reflecting
We are alive

In the birds and in the bees
Everything that breathes
In the woman and in the man
The earth and the sky
Belonging
We are alive

In the hours and in the days
Anything that stays
In the heart and in the soul
The earth and the sky
Believing
We are alive

In the summer and in the fall
No reason now to stall
In the winter and in the spring
These seasons will bring
The sun and the rain
Something profane
About the moon and the stars
Everything is ours

The earth and the sky
Revolving- We are alive

I drop my arm holding the page and simply… sit.

CHAPTER **12**

DOES ANYONE IN THIS WORLD REALLY KNOW WHAT THEY ARE SUPPOSED TO DO?

We all live in a paradox, a sci-fi episode for me at this point, where anything and everything is me against the present. The residue collects upon me and my endeavors, my dreams, leaving us to sit around and wonder should I or shouldn't I? But Nature just... is. Reminds me of the simplest solution is the best solution. I could have simply joined him on his little sojourn across his universe. But there is no rational argument for it. It's harmless wanting to wake up, put on a suit and tie, hit the machine of work, come home, have a beer, enjoy the earth and sky. But what if? Dammit, what if what I have is broken, possibly fatal? Like the futility of post-modernists, always wanting to deconstruct everything and re-construct to a skewed landscape of vanished aspiration. Admiration for the simplest pleasures is settling, compromising... flawed. Or... maybe his disclosure of life events, memories, poetry even, was the only way to reveal something new, a rebirth maybe? We all want to contribute, reveal something new and real, possibly even educate and inspire. But at what cost? Money is always an issue. Food is important to sustain. Guilt? Guilt is a cost. Should I feel guilty about insulting him, berating others?

"What the fuck!"

I get up and look both ways. Anyway is a good way. I start walking along the curb, mildly occupied by the growing water trail. Soap suds. A man washes his SUV in the driveway. He sees me and waves; I wave back. Must be his day off. Gotta wash the truck, make it look all spiffy. The things that entertain, pacify people. You've always been a cynic, haven't you? I dodge the largest water pile and continue walking in the exact middle of the street. I didn't realize I still carried his poem. I put it into my pocket. Reason: don't know, just because. I hate littering. Now which way?

It must have been forty minutes until I finally figured the way to the main street. I think it was forty minutes. You knew your phone was going to die if you called out- should've texted. Big shrug. Never realized how many kids like playing with the lawn sprinkler. Wanted to ask those kids if I could shoot a couple of baskets with them, but why? It doesn't matter now. I can't believe I just said that. The kids probably would have been afraid, or said yeah, feeling awkward, until one of them slipped away and told his mom. She probably would come out and yell, or even call the cops, and boom: in jail. I guess I can't fault her… or them. World is full of vile, lecherous, malicious, macabre people. Most are men too.

I finally get to a plaza which has a corner bar. I always enjoyed the atmosphere of a weekday crowd at a struggling dive of a cantina. The detection of sadness, odor of beer and fried food; the grizzled, gnarled faces of struggle scribbled upon their posture of the few people, men and women, who occupy at these times.

"Can I get a beer and a chilled whiskey double?"

The female bartenders are of an enigma that works at this time. The innumerable variables that constitutes their reason, or, more like need, to be here, serving predominantly men, older men, with their own reasons of being here. I learned long ago not to intrude upon a person's cloud at this moment. Less than half will respond with a reasonable answer; less than that will actually keep the conversation going. Most will kill it with the classic 'Yeah' and turn back to their thought or the muted TV with closed captioning. Even fewer will ask a question back. Sad.

"$9.50."

I get my wallet and find a lone ten dollar bill. Damn.

"Here."

She grabs it and already has the quarters in hand. With a clink and a clank they rest on the bar. Dead giveaway: she doesn't care to be here. Too bad. Her appearance can be easily improved to a better judgment of possible employers, improved pay, thus, improved outlook. I sip the shot and watch her go down the long bar back to a burning cigarette away from the four people in here.

The beer goes down quicker than I thought. Now comes the accounting. Did that check clear? Hmm. I put the bottle at the edge. She realizes after finishing a text and returns with a new one. I throw my credit card on the bar.

"Keep it open."

She turns around.

"Actually-"

She turns back to me. I blank out-

"Do you ever write poetry?"

The unknown of the reaction will always be a thrill. Discovering peoples' want, wishes... passions. She walks closer to me. Gotcha.

"I've read some but never thought about writing it."

"Well, may I ask why? Just for the simple reason of conversation and I think you have."

"I did. Many years ago."

Her facial expressions are still up in the air.

"Do you mind if I share a poem I wrote?"

She looks to the other patrons and sees they are

currently full.

"Sure… Go ahead."

I chuckle to myself. I pull out the notebook paper and begin.

"Earth and Sky-"

"Everybody stop. This man is a fraud!"

All heads turn to see Ted Christopher entering.

"This patron, if we can call him that, was about to deceive you!"

TC sits down next to me.

"Wow, can you believe this young pup was about to read you my song, for reasons undetermined, now what do you think about that?"

"He's an asshole then."

I can only smirk.

"Well, you can't prove that I wasn't going to improve upon this rough draft."

"Hah…. Debbie, could I get a bottled beer? Your choice."

She leaves with my first serving of constipation on her face.

"I have to hand it to you, kid. You are bold."

I drink my beer.

"What? Just making conversation. Cooling off with a beer."

"What was your motive, or more precisely, your agenda?"

Debbie returns with the beer.

"Put it on his tab"

She leaves without any intrigue to the charade that just played out.

"And she didn't want to hear it. Good job."

"How did you know I was in here?"

"Oh, call it luck, fate, predestination? Monyak and I followed you the entire walk here."

"You did? Fabulous."

"I knew you didn't make the right decision so I watched and observed. I just let you suffer in the shadows of your fragile mind."

I drink my beer. He drinks his. We become the rest of the patrons: silent.

"Okay. I'll jump first. How do you know?"

"Know what?"

"That I made a mistake."

"Oh, I don't know, per se, but I do know that there is more to be done. Finish your beer; I'll see you outside."

He tosses a twenty on the bar and walks out. I keep my stare straight ahead, analyzing the top half of my head in a framed mirror.

"Hey Debbie. Close it out with this."

I walk out. I stop and turn around and give her TC's poem.

"And keep this."

I exit and see TC putting in tobacco; the car idles in front. The sun shines bright, no wind, and still no good reason to go.

"No. I don't want to go home. I don't have a car and fuck, probably no job. Might as well, right?"

He nods and enters the car. I stand for a second, rationalize optimistically and get in. He sets two glasses on the console and throws in a couple of ice cubes. He opens a bottle of Johnny Walker Blue, hands me the glass and hits a button. The partition slides down. How did he get that damn console open?

"Monyak, 23981 Oak Brook Gardens North Royalton, apartment building #1103, just park behind the building."

The partition closes. I forgot to peer to the driver's seat to satisfy the mystery of the driver. I'm forgetting a lot.

"So what are you thinking? Just tell the truth."

"Nah. Not thinking. Just going with the flow."

TC closes the petition and pours another glass for me and him. He plays 'So Cruel,' by U2. We just sit and drink. The song ends right when the car parks.

"I met a girl, after college, and lived here. I spent six years with her. She was modeled after my high school sweetheart. She was five foot-one and less than a hundred pounds. She had the deepest blue eyes and long brown hair that stretched to the middle of her back. She had a smile, a way about her that made you feel loved. Her laugh was contagious. She was beautiful. Her name was Erica."

He runs his hand through his hair and scratches the back of his head.

"I had my grandmother's wedding ring... I just never gave it to her."

We exit the Lincoln and I follow him through the parking lot.

"The cops pulled me over here. I lived right there. My buddy was in the car. We had a few beers at the bar. I drove, it was wrong, but I was fine. The one cop wanted to just let me go. The other cop wanted to make a statement. He had his shiny badge, his black polished boots and shades. It was dark, no need for shades. After a series of tests I was arrested. Handcuffed and hulled away. I went to jail and lost my job at U.C.S. Erica went to work and I... I went insane."

He looks at the first floor, the last window. He reaches in his back pocket and hands me a folded sheet of paper.

"These words created my masterpiece. I lost everything and wrote this poem on the floor. I went crazy and scattered everything I have ever written. The living room was one large sanctuary of writing. Sit here on the curb; I'll be in the car waiting."

I'm getting quite accustom to these directions. I sit on

the curb and unfold this brittle piece of notebook paper. I read:

IN YOUR HONOR

slow red blood
trickling down like drops of rain
making music as they hit the floor
stripping away all the pain
of yesterday-

And yesterday
you were like a rose
ready to bloom
but now a dying flower
that came up to soon

And yesterday
you were like a violin
ready to be strung
to play a song
waiting to be sung

In your honor

Shakespeare has written
his final play
And Mozart has returned
for one last sonnet

In your honor

she wears a red dress
on this Sunday afternoon
her skin
illuminates the room-

And she is all you see
what you hoped for
and she is what you want
all you wrote before
has come true
Christopher
She's here for you

Lying beside you
comforting your pain
holding your hand
stopping the rain

In your honor

She pours the last glass of wine
and gives a toast

In your honor

An audience

Take a bow

For death
cannot be denied
Death
you cannot hide
from the devil
holding your soul inside

The love and his essential capacity to love invariably place a cold vibration over my internal core. His respective woes peel off with a dignity, valiance unfamiliar to me and my circle, friends and past relationships. The indifference in disrespecting these moments crystallizes inside my past writings, projects, dreams. I nod ever so slightly to the confirmation that I might learn something. But what is there to learn? I can't change the world in this hyper-kinetic slice of time, can I? I flush with a tinge of anger, shockingly, aimed at myself. I am a cynic. It's the last common denominator we all share in this bureaucratic, fickle libertarian state. Whew, what would I be like if I wasn't a cynic?

CHAPTER **13**

TO BE ALONE IS TO FAIL

I stand up, brush myself off and get back in the Lincoln.

"71 South, my good friend. You have the directions."

Partition goes up.

"Monyak is a good man. Crazy, unreliable, but wouldn't have it any other way. Here."

He hands me a framed picture of an ocean and some written words.

"This was a speech I delivered at my best friend's wedding."

He pours a couple of drinks. And he actually recites the speech as I read it.

BEST MAN SPEECH

Paul and I
Have known each other
For roughly twenty-years

From the backyard games
That later became high school football
To the grade school field trips
That turned into spring break

I can go on and on

But how can you sum up
A lifelong friendship

In a speech
It's impossible
For what is friendship?

It is the underlying feeling
That guys just don't talk about
They just know

I mean
You grow up
Where your parents decide to live
And you make friends
Along the way

But through life and experience
You only find a couple
You can call your best friends

For they possess
Certain qualities
Like honor, loyalty, and trust

The good friends
Have all these characteristics
Because no matter what happens in your life

Whether it is good or bad
They will be there for you

Thank you Paul
Thank you for always being there for me

Congratulations
May you and Karen be the greatest of lovers
And the best of friends.

The grandiloquence of the passion and the promise of

sincerity cannot be argued, or better stated, even denied. The strokes of his words are starting to meld within me. The direction and foresight he has is beginning to solidify with my current predicament. He hands me the drink and gives a toast.

"To friendship!"

"Agreed."

The Lincoln pulls onto the highway. TC searches through the music tracks.

"Sit back, relax, one last song and we can move on."

'Blowing in The Wind,' by Bob Dylan
blares from the speakers.

I relax, drink in hand and ingest the guitar, lyrics, timbre of Dylan's voice, and, I must admit, I feel content. Calmness has always been elusive for me but when I do get a sip of it, it's warm and luxurious because I do not know when it will return; because I can count on the buffoonery of worry and uncertainty pushing it down in the mud with impunity, making it seem delusional, possibly catatonic. I must attempt to unveil the shadow he employs on this convoy. Nervousness is controlled by the moderation of sauce; however, there is always the kick-back from getting too close. TC sits back with his eyes closed until the song ends.

"Intensity and passion coupled with inspiration and promotion. You have experienced some of the parts to the sum, congratulations. Now we can move on."

I shake the cubes with anxious attention. He blurts with adamancy.

"Never forget that picture of the ocean and that speech."

TC hits the divider:

"Monyak, are we on schedule?"

"Yes, we'll be in Chicago in less than six hours."

The divider closes, TC pours another drink.

"I can't stress this enough. But one of the key elements in life is friendship. Sit back and enjoy your drink and just listen... to the world spinning."

I sit back with a full Crown and attempt. Immediately, it's lost to the reality of my life... I try again... frustrated, angered, I peep at TC. He sits and stares out the window. At what?! So I look: the Ohio turnpike, farmland, cows graze; hay lies in bundles upon a field, a young farm-hand starts his duty. I instantaneously give him props for his routine.

My reflective diligence breaks for an interruption:

"I grew up in a suburban town, Forest Hills, in Medina County. Everyone seems to associate Ohio with farms. It makes me laugh. I lived in a place where no one was rich and no one was poor, just the average American family; in an average American suburban town... just ask, c'mon, I'm not too old..."

My ice-cubes clink as they melt; a screech of tires, back to normal-

"Three of my best friends growing up were Pat, Mike and Lewis. Pat was the youngest of five, Lewis the youngest of seven, Mike and I the youngest of three. You can pretty much say that we grew up faster than we should have."

TC sits back and laughs; I toss in more ice and put on a seatbelt, arrogantly pissed that this is all routine... for him. A slight ping of selfishness flits in my head.

"Pat was an intelligent kid: reading 'A Clockwork Orange', by Anthony Burgess for fun in fifth grade. He liked wearing college t-shirts, wrestling shoes and a pair of jeans. On the playground, I would pick him first, because I could throw up a Hail Mary and know that somehow he would come down with it. He was a solid kid, with hints of gray in his hair. At the age of ten, isn't that crazy?"

Interesting to him but not to me... he looks at me, so I just agree and shake my head.

"Mike was the type of kid who had a collection of dirty mags underneath his bed. Not the type of gentleman's mag that you would rummage through your dad's closet and find. He was definitely unique; into GQ, the latest fashion and the underground music scene. Every year was different for him. One year he would be a punk; the next year a jock, and a year later, a prep. So it did not surprise me to hear about his sleeve tattoos. He searched out the greatest artist in Canada to do his left arm and the greatest artist in Europe for his right arm. His right sleeve, I believe, is the Four Horseman of the Apocalypse. Mike was always a great artist. He helped draw the design."

He cracks open the red-felt bag containing a bottle of Grand Marnier. He throws in a few cubes of ice and pours a glass. He takes a tiny straw and stirs up the liquor. I could be somewhere else but I can't find an appropriate substitution: I relax more to the drink, the car ride, his words...

"Lewis, we were inseparable. He was smart but normal. He liked video games and sports. His father, a great man, loved watching the Browns, the Indians, the Cavaliers and the Buckeyes. Lewis was a great athlete: tough and rugged. The type of kid you wanted on your team, no matter what sport you were playing. What a leader! Someone to look up to, someone you did not mind to follow."

He sets the straw on the ledge behind him and sips from the glass.

"We were all followers of one another, but at the same time leaders of each other."

I remember walking the school hallways with the same veneer: owning the school, doing whatever my friends and I wanted. Too bad that was in eighth grade.

"A normal Saturday Night in middle school for us, was walking up Skyview Hill and hitting up the restaurant. Back then a cigarette machine could be found in the doorway. We would buy a pack of Camel Lights that came with a book of matches and smoke. We would take a different route home and sing lyrics from 'Appetite for Destruction' by Guns n Roses. We would eventually reach 1107 Claremont and instantly walk past the kitchen and down to the basement. In the fridge would be a case or two of beer. The rotary phone would ring and one of our girlfriends would be calling from the skate station. Yes, we were stupid. But you know what- we were living. And creating a bond that no one will ever be able to break! The four of us would hold up our beers and drink until we passed out."

He stares out the window. I just can't listen free of void in the senseless joy; I have to contemplate about myself. For once, I internally tell myself to continue listening: always in such a rush. Why am I always in such a rush?

"Pat and Lewis ended up going to St. Ignatius High School in Cleveland. Lewis became a great swimmer and Pat was a state finalist in wrestling. From there they went to Ohio University in Athens, Ohio. I visited Lewis a couple of times around Halloween. He was the president of the Sigma Chi fraternity. Lost touch with Pat, but heard he would party and not study and still ace his way through chemical engineering school. Lewis graduated with a civil engineering degree and landed a lucrative job in Chicago. Pat moved to San Francisco and made it big. Mike and I went to Brunswick High. We played football and both went to Akron University. Mike grew out his hair; he looked like Brad Pitt in an 'Interview with a Vampire.' Then one day he buzzed his head and joined the Marine Corp. He guarded a few embassies around the world and met two Presidents. I think Bush and Clinton. He finished his Russian studies degree in Houston and now works underground for the government. Top secret kind of shit, last I heard he was in Africa."

TC sits up and packs a tin of Kodiak. He places a healthy sized dip in his bottom lip and grabs an empty Gatorade bottle. I take a hint and light up a smoke. He lounges in his seat, shaking his head and laughing.

"Paul, Travis, John and Ron. It's strange how friends become best friends at different points in life. Paul! Remember the best man speech? Well, Paul was a tough kid. He wore Army t-shirts and loved to play football, wrestle and fight. His father loved the Steelers and the steel curtain, so of course he did. We used to call each other up, 225-****; I can't believe I remember his number. Amazing, we would meet in the field on top of the hill and play one on one football. I would juke and fake and sometimes get around him. He would just lower his head and run full steam ahead. It was like tackling a bull dozer. Funny shit, we probably played this stupid game about a thousand times. We should have just flipped a coin and said you win, you lose. Paul was the strongest kid on our high school team. He had hillbilly strength and such a burning passion to hit someone. He was a good guy to have on your side."

TC runs his hand through his hair and laughs. I should buy a new phone. The pure randomness of my mind is spawning.

"Oh shit, next is Travis. I met Travis in seventh grade. He was already six-foot three, with a blonde hair mullet and glasses. A gangly fuck, just a goof! He wore a black leather studded bracelet and thought it made him look cool. To be honest he ended up working out and turned out to be like Drago, from the movie Rocky. My friends and I knew him better. He was Travis, the type of person that could understand Einstein and the theory of relativity, yet believe that Forrest Gump was still alive."

I envision these characters and just laugh as TC stares out the window, probably collecting his next installment. I have a gnawing wonder what they are doing now, surprising myself.

"John. I met him in eighth grade. He had this patch covering his left eye. No, he was not a pirate; he was an idiot that caught his eyelid on a garage door. He loved sports and being in the center of the action. He became our high school quarterback and fit the part wearing number 13 to honor his childhood hero. I must admit, he did look like Dan Marino. John! He was the type of guy that could not go a day without a girlfriend. He would fix his crew cut that never did move and flirt with cheerleaders. I give him credit; he seized the moment and went out with the best looking girls in the school."

He spits out his chew, grabs a Budweiser this time and lounges back in the leather seat.

"Ron, fucking Ron. I met him through Travis, my freshman year in college. He was all of 300 pounds, an offensive lineman at the University. I can't remember if the team was even good. It doesn't matter; it's still Division One football. Bottom line: Travis said he was cool. So, in our book, he was cool, and, after I got to know him, he was cool. He fit right in. You know why?"

I give the obligatory shrug.

"Because friendship is not just about drinking; it's about- it's about staying up all night and revealing your dreams, your insecurities. Put it this way. I'm glad I knew him, because later on he became the bartender at the best bar in Akron. Man, I got to fuckin' piss."

He hits the button and the divider comes down.

"Monyak, pull over."

We pull over on the side of the highway. It's something in the morning. The interim of passing cars collide with the serenity of silence and peace around me. I always thought about the nature of things to a point where my impulsiveness led me down another crooked route... and now I'm here. We all exit the car: TC and Monyak piss on the trees, while I piss with the thought of a raccoon or other creature being awoken by a stream and attacking where... I am the most vulnerable. Monyak finishes first.

"What the fuck, man. It's Notre Dame. Respect that shit. Don't piss on that sign."

We jump back in the Lincoln. Thank God it's dark outside. The dribble on my jeans is not a good thing. Never rush a man in mid-stream.

"Monyak, when we get to Chicago, park the car and let us sleep."

"No problem."

The divider closes. TC hits the compartment and throws me a blanket and a pillow. He grabs his own blanket and lies down to sleep.

"Get some sleep. Tomorrow will be interesting."

I guess I'm tired, but I need to dwell on other things than guys in my head. Eighth grade comes into view: the innocence of thinking only of the end of the school day was the concern. I set myself up to spin on the myriad thoughts of the past couple of days and the ripple effects yet to come. An hour goes by until the hum of the car puts me out.

CHAPTER **14**

A NIGHT WHERE THE PAST MEETS THE PRESENT {RECKLESS YOUTH}

I awake at 2:30 in the afternoon: damn tinted windows and cloudy skies, I hate sleeping this late. I walk outside and see TC in Millennium Park: tourists walk about; children play in the Crown Fountain. Half awake, I walk over and see him writing with a little golf pencil. He crumbles up the piece of paper he writes on and throws it in my direction.

"I don't know, just read it. It took about ten minutes. I'll be in the car."

I stop watching the co-existence of people and grab the crumbled sheet from the ground. I unfold it and read:

IT WAS BEAUTIFUL

My first memory
Was the 1980
U.S hockey team
I was 5

I had-
Two older sisters
And a mother
And a father

I was raised-
To be strong

I had-
A fort
A place I could be
On my own

I had-
Friends
-Moments
-They were like brothers

I had-
A girl
That was more-
-Than a friend

LIFE
IT WAS BEAUTIFUL

I held a football
Scored a touchdown
And went out with a cheerleader
I went to prom
Got drunk
Sang a song
And passed out

I went to college
Joined a fraternity
Got drunk
And failed out

LIFE

I left Cleveland
And searched... And searched

I went to New Orleans

And felt the Jazz

I went to Woodstock in New York
And felt the 60's

I went to Venice in L.A
And lived like a rock star
For months

I went to Vegas
And snatched 15 girls from Chicago
And took them back to my room
For a night

IT WAS BEAUTIFUL

I drank hard liquor
And hung out in strip clubs
I did drugs
And crashed out in unknown places
For what-

-Fame
-Fortune
-The experience

I went back to Cleveland
And walked the midnight street
In solace

So I went to a church
And knelt beneath the crucifix
And prayed

I woke the next morning
And went to a cemetery
Where I sat at my friend Kenny's grave

And realized
How wonderful it is-
-To be alive

So I went to the woods
And sat against a tree
And wrote

LIFE
IT IS BEAUTIFUL

Ted Christopher

Dedicated to Kenny K.
My lifelong friend and college roommate

(We will never be as innocent as the day we were born.)

The loss of a friend: a schism in a person's young life; the instability breeds shattered images of invincibility. I remember a friend I lost. We had a song that we would listen to before we started our weekend of beers and loud music. Call it an anthem or oafish as some has said, but it still gets me every time I hear "Damage Inc." by Metallica. That was our duo's brand. We would live our separate lives but made a pact that whenever we got a phone call and the other end came a whisper 'Damage Inc.', we would drop what we were doing and meet up to become the debaucheries of modernity. I never got the call but instead a call from his cousin with the news. He died in July. His name was Tom.

I get in the Lincoln. The divider is open with 'Yahweh', by U2, blaring from the speakers. We drive into the heart of downtown Chicago. TC just smiles as we sit in traffic. The song ends. He speaks to Monyak, as he looks down at the directions.

1346 Southport Avenue - Apt 4R. It's on the Northwest corner of Southport and Roscoe, immediately next to the Southport Brown Line stop."

He looks at me and starts laughing; his creativity in living agitates me.

"Well, I hope you are ready to drink."

I take it back. Nothing like a new day to enjoy sauce, letting the sun shine on you, giving meaning to shapes and symbols that were otherwise buried by our deliberate function of life. There is no clear reason or academic catalyst for this spark. The Lincoln pulls to the side of the road.

"We're here. You guys have fun. I'll be here tomorrow. Don't die."

Really? I shake it off as another over-dramatic statement from the two that has turned into my impromptu tribe. We exit the car and walk pass people dining on the patio at a place called Ann Sather's. Directly above this little bistro is Apartment 4R. We walk the steps and knock on the front door. A man answers the door in a pair of army green shorts and an Ohio University t-shirt.

"Theo!"

"Lewis, what the fuck is going on man?"

They shake hands; we enter. TC introduces me as his personal stenographer. Lewis just looks at me.

"He's always been strange."

Lewis takes us on a tour of the four bedrooms and the two and half baths. A foosball table sits in the corner of the living room with three couches and a 52" television. TC is lit up with excitement. His mysterious age does not shed from his gaiety.

"Where is everybody?"

"Mike and Pat are at Newport Bar and Grill, bullshitting with Old Sal. Travis and Ron are down the street at a bar called Justin's."

We take the steps to his loft and walk out onto a deck that overlooks train tracks and an open area with a basketball hoop. TC leans over the railing.

"You two fucks are a disgrace!"

Two guys stop their game. I follow Lewis downstairs. He grabs a few Budweiser's from the fridge.

"I bought six cases of beer, do you think that will be enough?"

"Maybe?"

Paul and John enter the house all sweaty and go right for the fridge. Ron and Travis enter the house talking about some hot bartender. Mike and Pat enter with a similar conversation. I decide to stand in the background and blend. It is fleetingly eerie that no one acts much older than me. I shake it off looking for a seat but catch these guys not slapping hands or doing some crazy ritual greeting- they just shake hands, crack beers and drink. No one sits down; there goes my chance. They lean against the table, the couch, the foosball table and TV stand. Lewis comes out of the kitchen with a jug of red wine.

"To Theo... Happy birthday however long ago it was!"

I reach for my phone out of habit. The guys gather around in a circle. They chug as much as they can and pass it on. Ron calls me in to the mix. I chug as much as I can and pass it to the next guy. The jug makes its way to TC. He polishes off the bottle and lets out a loud relief.

"All I need now... is Paul's wife and I'll be good."

"You're an asshole. I know you took her to prom."

"Yeah, and didn't do anything with her. Not even a kiss-brother."

Mike starts throwing everybody beers. I catch mine and still wonder about their routine. Are they still in college? I actually shrug to myself. Paul steps up.

"I would pay this dick head to write my papers in…"

TC jumps in.

"First period, Brit Lit with Mrs. Di'Tommasco."

"I never read what the fucker wrote; he would just take my ten dollars and tell me I just got another A. At the end of the year, Mrs. D called me into her office and asked me why I relate every heroine to my girlfriend."

TC chugs his beer and stands in front of everybody.

"The best was when I was with Paul's future wife at Greg's house. Greg gave my buddy Rob the keys and said just clean up before we get back from vacation. Paul, Pat, Rob and I drank over five cases of beer in like three days. Greg's parents called the cops on us. God forbid a little warning. I was with Karen, your future wife Paul, Rob was with his girlfriend. We were just sitting at the table, not even drinking."

TC laughs uncontrollably when he remembers past events. I wonder how much he's laughed this year.

"All of a sudden, this unknown woman comes in from the back door with Tom and Jerry. It was like a cartoon, her and the good old Brunswick Police Department! Paul for some reason just ran out the front door. He made it to the hill behind my house, before he got tackled."

Paul chimes in.

"I took the fall for you man."

"Sure you did. Fucking Paul said he just drank the Busch Light! We had a mountain of beer cans, no pun intended, stacked up in the basement. Ninety-eight percent was Busch Light. So I said I drank the Busch. I still got arrested."

Mike hints he needs one; he nods to me if I need another one. I shake him off. He joins the group.

"Greg- unbelievable. Ted and I went with him to Woodstock in '94. He drove his parents Cadillac. We were in college, experimenting with drugs and that kind of shit. We didn't have a tent or any place to sleep. Just drank and got wasted until we passed out. It all got fucked up. I couldn't find Greg or Ted; well, I did find Ted, this asshole, was sliding down some hill with a bunch of hippies. He was covered in mud."

I decide on getting involved.

"How the fuck did you get home?"

"We held signs on some highway in New York. A station wagon with a bunch of guys and girls from Kent State pulled over and drove us home. I was flipping out. Ted didn't care."

The big guy, Ron, drums up his own mantra.

"Ted never cared. I remember meeting Mike and Travis at Brown, that shitty dorm behind Bobb-A-Louies. There was an actual line that divided their room. Mike's side was organized, the bed was made, and his clothes perfectly folded. Travis' was a mess; he used his bed post as a spitter and had dirty clothes all over the place. I met John, Paul and Ted a few months later on Allen Street. They threw parties and liked to get fucked up. It was all fucking great."

Paul throws everyone a beer; I catch it and notice I am done, but John starts laughing.

"I remember coming home between algebra and speech class and seeing Teddy smoking weed with our roommate, Phil. Not just a joint. He's clearing a four-foot bong and smoking a pipe. Stoned out of his mind, he grabs a candle and places it in a red-felt Grand Marnier bottle and walks out the front door. I just follow this dumb ass and shake my head. We get to class and it's his turn to give a speech. He has me turn off the light. It's silent- pitch black. He strikes a match and lights the candle. I stand in the back of the room and try not to laugh. He is up there reciting poetry by Jim Morrison. He finishes, so I turn on the light. The students are dumbfounded, just asking if Jim Morrison did drugs. Teddy can barely fucking stand let alone answer a question about drugs."

I draw attention to myself by holding up a pack of smokes and a lighter.

"You guys are fucking unbelievable. I need to step outside and have a smoke."

The guys and TC acknowledge quickly, going back into their loud chat, the glass sliding door relieves the noise, for a new noise of city chatter and traffic jams: a new balm for my ears. I light my smoke and look out, feeling here but not. My intuition always creeps in earlier than I want. It feeds off my uncertainty but I do the same thing I always do: push my trash compactor mind to compress it. I look out into the cityscape but notice a fortune cookie on the deck. I don't eat that garbage but find the over-ripe fortunes worth the effort. The cookie-that-was-not-meant-to-be-eaten reads:

IN THE PROVINCE OF THE MIND, WHAT ONE BELIEVES
TO BE TRUE EITHER IS TRUE OR BECOMES TRUE.

I toss the fortune over the edge and instantly reach for it, not wanting to litter. Then my eyes wander on a hot-dog vendor on the corner. I watch. This man who sits in a cheap, white plastic patio chair rests simply with his hands folded over his over-sized pot belly. His demeanor can only be ambiguous; it's too far to see his face. What a sight I think. This man probably comes out every morning in this Chicago weather pan-handling lunches for people who can afford anything. His cart is decorated with ribbons, umbrella, and hand-made signs with poor graphics. I sum him up as a soldier of capitalism. Is this because I am in Chicago? Is that what I am: a soldier? A defunct, AWOL soldier to my lifestyle of standing in line for a hand-out of the liberal? This trip has unearthed many deep boxes of unconscious, underground treats that will not go away as I try to swat them away. These flies of destiny and impressionistic fears cannot be ignored forever. This trip will explode within me if I do not say something. The smoke has run its span and I toss it over the edge, but to the side, and enter back in the glass sliding doors. The noise within explodes from everyone talking at once. I stand closer to the group wanting another beer as the guys just chug beer after beer. Cans are beginning to line the living room.

"Fucking college! I let Teddy borrow my car one morning to get a tin of Kodiak. Four hours later, I'm sitting there without dip, without a car, just wondering where the fuck he went."

TC stands up and dramatically calms the group down like a quarterback on a two-minute drill.

"Okay... Travis and I were hammered the night before. I could barely open my eyes the next morning. I grab a few tins of chew, which I paid for you- cheap mother fucker- and get in his Trans Am, that 1970's hard rock muscle car that of course Balboa drove in what- Rocky III. Beneath the fucking eagle hood was a corvette engine. I'm driving down Market St. I miss fucking Wheeler or Allen and make a quick turn down Kling. Right in front of Kinko's, I hit the gas, the spitter spills on the passenger seat and all of a sudden, I'm on the fucking sidewalk. A witness said I ran up the telephone wire and flipped the car about eight feet in the air. I landed on the t-tops, my fucking tiny ass head was in that little section. The roof was crushed to the dashboard. The jaws-of-life came. It was funny; I crawled through this tiny opening and saw about a hundred people in the street. I guess it was my moment of fame. I walked around the car and asked the fireman if everything was alright! He was crouched down looking in the car. You should have seen his face. I just said I was fine, no big deal. The tires on the car were still spinning, I don't even know if I turned off the engine. Shit, three days later, John and I won the flag football championship. Akron sent our team 'The Plague' down to New Orleans, and we get crushed."

"Dude! I saw that fucking car. I don't know how you didn't die?"

"Who the fuck knows, Paul... I don't know, I guess some people are not meant to die."

"How many cars did you wreck? I know you bent the axle on the Probe. God, we were wasted. You hit a curb or something?"

"It was your fucking fault man! Ron hits me on the arm to look at some bitch coming out of a bar. Two seconds later, I jumped the curb and fucked up the car. It wasn't the first time; I wrecked my parent's car when I was fourteen."

I stand around and just say 'Fuck it' and grab a beer. Pat cracks a beer and joins the conversation.

"Yeah, Teddy and I crashed on Skyview. We hit a snow bank and took out a mail box. We were digging the snow out with our hands. This guy, with a wife and two little kids in the back, jumps out and helps. He saw the empty beer cans and got us out of there. We had no idea what to do. We broke into your house, Lewis, and tried to warm up. Teddy's fingers were blocks of ice. We both got frost bite that night. I guess it was better than getting arrested."

John chimes into the conversation:

"How about Travis and Mike drag racing down Magnolia? Mike is driving a CRX and Travis is driving his uncle's corvette?"

"Travis couldn't stay in his lane."

"It was your fault, man! You knew I was pulling away so you side swiped me."

"All I remember is the speedometer at 95 and then spinning and flipping into that lawn! Barely missing a tree!"

"I don't know how the fuck we survived."

TC paces among the group and waits for it to calm down before he speaks. I simply... am looking forward to where this is going.

"Yeah... Paul wrecked my car. I'm tripping on acid at some bonfire and Paul, sober, is limping towards the fire, screaming: I wrecked your car. We go back to his house. You know Senior Rock, Paul is getting the keys to his dad's car to go to the hospital. His dad, in a damn Steelers sweatshirt, is just shaking his head. I'm so pale and wasted that I'm telling his dad that I never drank so much alcohol in my life, just so he wouldn't think I was on drugs. Paul is in the emergency room for about four hours, probably like forty minutes. I don't know- there was a father and a few kids in the waiting room, worried about their mother- if she was going to die or be alive. I'm hitting my peak and I can completely feel their anxiety and sadness. I walk outside to get away and run into a cop. I don't know, Tom – Jerry, who knows? He's asking about some car. I have no clue where the fuck I am. I just talked to his father; I'm at the hospital and talking to a cop. That was not a great night."

Lewis brushes past me and comes out of the kitchen with a beer bong. I just sit back and watch these old guys crack beers and tilt bong. I totally forget who is who.

"Fucking Teddy! My brother and I threw our annual summer bash. My mom for some reason was in the kitchen.

She's freaking out. Johnny and I are just trying to calm her down. She looks out the back window and sees Teddy doing three beers in a bong. She starts yelling: everyone is wasted! People are puking and Teddy is drinking out of a funnel. Aww- so much stupid shit."

I decide it's time for another smoke break when someone grabs my shoulder to hold on, pulling out his dentures at the same time. Mike speaks.

"Travis, what the fuck were you thinking?"

I look with simple shock, and, to be honest, curiosity. Travis laughs like the villain in Highlander.

"I just thought a cement saw would cut wood. The fucking thing kicked back and drilled me in the face. It didn't even fucking hurt. I just walked back to the work site. The foreman at the time just said get in the fucking truck and don't even try to look in the mirror. A hundred and fifty stitches and a few months of plastic surgery put me back together. I was pretty much mangled just like my Trans Am, asshole."

Their back-and-forth is dizzying; I wonder if my co-workers miss me.

Ron, cracking a beer and laughing; "A few months later, Travis is at Heinz field, flicking a cigarette and blowing up a propane tank." John, cracking another beer; "That sounds like Travis."

Thank God, a cell-phone rings to break up this rhinoceros fest. John, the Ohio State guy, answers and leaves the room. The guys razz him a bit as he leaves. I think Paul just finished a bong; he walks away holding his stomach. I follow him carefully, knowing where this might end. In the adjacent room, he squirms on the bed. 'No Woman, No Cry' by Bob Marley plays on the stereo. Travis tries to yell over the music.

"I'm going to puke."

CHAPTER **15**

THE QUESTION IS NOT WHY WE ARE HERE. THE QUESTION IS: WHAT MAKES LIFE WORTH LIVING?

I smirk to myself: a bunch of old men keeping the college lifestyle alive.

"Dude, just fucking puke... it's easy."

The guy relaxing on a lounge chair revels in the entire bit.

"If you're going to puke, puke on me."

Before I knew it, Travis sticks a few fingers down his throat and pukes all over Pat. Paul, in the bedroom, screams in anguish. TC, laughing so hard, runs to the balcony and pukes over the railing. I just watch the entire scene and wonder if these guys have ever been sober. Or even worse: is this how I act when I'm drunk? I wanted to smoke but... why? The guy who owns the place just laughs and throws the puked-on guy some new clothes. They crack more beers and continue to party. I'm in awe. These guys are unbelievable! I could not imagine them in their prime, let alone if I was puked on or if it was my place. They partied on. Last I checked my watch it was about seven in the morning. I finally passed out on the deck.

I slept on and off. Finally, I moved inside to a couch that someone inadvertently left alone. As the prowler I am, I snatched and acted like I was asleep. The groans and grunts of the prey were priceless knowing he had lost his spot.

By the time I came out of my cocoon it was about 8:30 in the evening. The names came easier today: the owner of the place set two garbage containers in the middle of the living room; the puker and the pukee were not seen. The rest of the people took about 10 minutes throwing away all the cans. The place looked pretty much spotless. TC and I shook hands with everybody and left the apartment. Monyak was ready with the Lincoln: the first time I've been so happy to see it. TC, a little disgruntled, tells Monyak to drive to the park. He sits on the edge of the seat with his elbows resting on the top of his knees and his eye sockets in the palm of his hands.

I look at him, wondering if his old age has clouded his mind. He just smirks, knowing something, but never revealing it.

"Are you alright?"

"Ron lives in New York. Paul in Michigan. John in Cleveland. Pat in San Francisco. Travis in Cincinnati and Mike lives in Africa. They all flew in for last night. That is friendship: they all knew, didn't say a thing. I'm a lucky man."

"You should be."

"But I'm not, they're all married… and I'm alone."

He rubs his hands over his face, sniffles and looks up at the ceiling. I'm surprised at the doleful words and think that his life is one that will never be understood; just a mission minus the accomplishment. I think he will die in sorrow. Thoughts of the same thing ring in my ears when I reach for my cell-phone: I need to go home and get back into that routine I so abhor. Now if that's not nonsense, what is? Big sigh.

The Lincoln pulls into North Park Village and parks. TC grabs a postcard and exits the car. I stay in the car and watch him sit on a park bench. He just sits there and stares at the moon. After about ten minutes, I get out of the car and walk over to him. He has a tear in his eye as he hands me the post card.

"It's to my high school sweetheart."

I look at a crystal clear picture of Wrigley Field. I turn the post card over and read:

Allie,

I let you in. I let you know how I feel
I never let anyone in. I never let anyone
    know how I felt
Thank You – Thank You
It feels so good
To let your guard down – To open up
To speak the truth – To be free
To not care what the world thinks
To be completely who you are
But most of all
To love
And to say it to the one you love

Allie,
I love you

Forever – I miss you
Teddy

137

I follow him back and get in the Lincoln.

"Denver, Colorado, Monyak."

I think about how crazy all of this has become. The divider closes and 'Creep' by Radiohead begins to play. We take a few side streets and get onto I-88 West. The song ends. And in that moment of silence, I wonder where this road will take me and if I can change, if I can be someone different. I wonder if this is a waste of my time. Is any of this worth it?

'Time to Say Good-Bye' by Brightman and Boccelli follows, blaring with intensity from the speakers. I look out the window and see the city of Chicago on fire: the sunset against the skyscrapers builds layers upon acres of smoke stacks and factories and ambivalent buildings. TC just smiles at the site of it all. I find it fitting: leaving a house on fire, leaving a city on fire. This guy's got something.

The car ride is simple: no words and, for a brief hiatus, no thoughts. I can only assume last night did some damage. The headache I have is absolutely splitting my cranium with a vexation. I barely function let alone care since I only want to be simple and raw, understood and right. I figure the best route for me, since the last sign I see is Des Moines, is to rest. If Utopia is where I'm heading, I need some sleep, especially if I can get back to a dream with normalcy: I'll take anything-even a dream of being at work...

> Berlin was a city, a shotglass appears, I drink.
> Be there at 9am or be a Phoenix,
> I reach the AP Foodmart for no bus arrives,
> Pogo around as my ride wonders on the
> Arrangement,
> Cuckle, cookoo, cocoa, I hear
> Is the words. Or the empty
> Symbols, leaving me behind a wheel
> Where I have no teeth, teeth to

Reciprocate, to refabricate, to
Re-upholster, I sit on the curb.

I'm jolted awake by a large pot-hole. The ramblings still fall from my ear as decayed wax. I happily look at my watch to see twelve hours have gone by but it's only been three hours when a take a second look. The landscape outside is as barren as my hope for sleeping again. TC snores; the resistance to wake him befuddles me. Why can't I wake him? What am I to do now? I re-adjust my posture and close my eyes again.

Did you get that ride?
Who are you?
I'm Pablo, this is Piet, you know,
And what is that writhing thing?
That's your Liver,
Heads Up!
The cards are shuffled and laid flat,
Texas Hold'Em my friend,
My writhing liver, burps,
I gag, my cards, I can't read,
Pablo nudges me,
If Utopia is what you want, atomize it.
What, Piet, throws down a cardboard heart
Flush!
I can't read my cards,
No worry, use your Legs,
I try to run...

I wake up desiring this independence of reality: and it, the first sight, is TC throwing in a dip.
"Rise and shine, Pumpkin- we're in Lincoln, Nebraska!"
I shake my head from the remnants of my last thoughts. Whatever happened to dreams of flying or running or

anything that can be found in the farce of a dream dictionary? I look at my glass of Crown and think twice. Nope, this is real. TC heads to the quick mart as Monyak gases the car.

"Hey, Monyak, why did you do this gig?"

He looks down, shaking his head.

"It's worth it. Trust me, it's worth it."

I simply stare at him and do not respond or act to his rhetoric. I feel collapsed upon; I'm trying to too hard. I think it's time not to think. I go back in the car and try to relax. I can't. So the next best thing for me to do is to breathe... no, slower. If only I had the choice of music right now I would bounce back into the rhythm, the lyrics...

TC gets in the Lincoln and sits back in his seat, packing his new tin. It's silent for hours; I didn't bother to ask, or rather, question the way he feels; I let him sip his drink and stare at what remains of the moon from the window. The sun is appearing. I just smoke a few cigarettes; I didn't refrain from my Crown either. He decides now to play music from his console. Enya comes on: I merely close my eyes and think about the friends I left behind. TC was able to re-connect with his: will I have the chance to?

"You shared some trivial stories back there in Chicago."

"No. It was nothing more than a recollection; just a reality of what makes life worth living."

"Was it a good decision to recall those moments? Your friends traveled all over the world to see you."

TC doesn't break his stare. I'm guessing the moon is outside his window.

"If you got something to say, say it to me now."

I place the empty glass down and feel off-guard. I do have something to say but the recoil of his words springs back down into the recesses of my gut. I shift, stammer, stumble over words, articles, and get nothing.

"When you have what you want to say- then say it. If not, okay."

I restrain myself from wasting the moment and changing the inconvenience of this into a cloud of my own. The chords of Enya's composure are fitting for my lack of rant.

The rest of the way was uneventful for anyone who has had to drive through Nebraska. The journey has as much diversity as miles of cornfields, soybeans, and wheat in one. My conflict with being out of touch with my family and friends begin to weigh on me.

"We need to go to a store so I can get a new phone."

TC laughs; the divider goes down with his thumb at me. Monyak sees the entire scene in the rear view mirror. I feel stupid as Monyak's eyes say 'What?' but what else can I do?

"Monyak, could we stop at a retail place, outlet, whatever: I need a phone."

"To be honest, it might put us behind schedule. Haven't you learned anything? If you don't have a phone then you don't have to be responsible."

"It's okay, Monyak. We can stop at a pet store and get him a leash."

The divider rises; I have to laugh at the sophomore humor TC attempts but it is what it is.

"A leash? Being linked with people you care about and understand is called a leash?"

TC laughs.

"It's part of life. Everyone needs someone. It's the nature of things to be liked, loved... appreciated."

"You may have missed some opportunities, but I haven't. I'm sorry that your friends are scattered all over this world. I'm sorry that you never realized your dream. I'm sorry that love has slipped through your fingers. I'm sorry, but where is your high school sweetheart if she's your love?"

The vulnerable flinch of TC causes me to regret; no retreat for my speech.

"Kid, you stepped over the line."

I see the sorrow in his eye. I feel stupid. He looks at me so defiantly and I understand. His iron gaze is warranted.

"I'm sorry. It was an assumption, not an assault."

Monyak pulls up to the front doors.

"I know, let's get this fucking mall over with and get you a cell phone."

"It's a freaking mall, TC."

"Yeah, a graveyard to me."

We enter the glass doors and the activity is robust for being so early. I simply start scanning immediately for a kiosk or a store. TC lazily wanders behind me with his arms cupped behind his back as if in a stroll through a park, or maybe a graveyard? Odd association, I tell myself.

"C'mon, if you want to get this over, you can pick up the pace."

"I am going as fast I can."

I find the store and wait for a clerk. TC stands off in the corner and stares at some literature, seemingly afraid to enter any further into this cave of a predator. I continue and speak with the clerk.

"If I could cash in on my upgrade, also change over my phone numbers, please." The clerk and his ten dollar pitch answers.

"We have an assortment of rebates available if you'd like to pay fifty dollars."

"Just give him a leash with some spikes on it."

TC laughs at his own joke.

"Never mind him; I'm just looking for a similar one to this for no charge and a transfer of numbers."

"I would like to ask if there is any need for the internet on your phone? We have-"

"The world wide web? How intriguing, so you can not only be leashed but caged."

The patience of this clerk is ebbing from his ears, I can see it. I've been in his shoes.

"When you get this type of job, nothing makes sense but cream cheese for breakfast and prunes for dinner."

The clerk looks up at TC, so I point back at him.

"Don't pay attention to him, he still trying to figure out call waiting."

The clerk enjoys the quip; he goes back to find a phone and paperwork.

"I'll be back in a second."

TC picks up a phone.

"Look, all the phones even foreshadow what you're getting involved with."

He tries to take a phone from the shelf but it's tethered to the display.

"Really? We have a child amongst us. It's tied down for theft or even worse, old codgers like you trying to bring back Morse code."

TC puts it back on the rack and exits the store. I finish what I'm doing and join him outside the mall.

"See it didn't take long at all. Now we can go."

Monyak pulls up the Lincoln.

"Communication is not a cell phone."

"Of course not, either are family dinners."

He just shakes his head, laughs and gets in the car. I look back at the mall and all the people shopping. Maybe when this is over and I'm broke and homeless, I could still get a job in the mall: the land of the American dream.

CHAPTER **16**

WHAT IS NECESSARY MAY NOT ALWAYS BE NECESSARY

I make all my phone calls outside this mall in Nebraska feeling unbalanced. I open the door to get in the car. TC's hand stops me.

"Dude, you fucking stink. Here's two-hundred dollars. Go get some fucking clothes and deodorant."

"And you don't?"

"You have ten minutes."

I slam the door and jog back in the mall. I grab two pairs of jeans, two t-shirts and a Michigan sweatshirt. This has to be the first piece of collegiate wear I ever bought. I just liked the fabric and the price was outrageous. Seventy dollars: not my money. I run down the escalator, grab deodorant, toothpaste and a toothbrush at a boutique drugstore. A line of people with the same pattern of random items as the people holding them; I look down at my watch. Still got time so might as well use the phone.

I jump into the car wearing a new T-shirt and jeans since it was slowly driving away with an open door. We get back on the highway to the nascent of the omnipotent mountains. They will begin to fill the horizon with strength and majesty. He doesn't ask about my clothing choices so I bring up something else.

"I made all my phone calls back home."

TC leisurely sits, looking at me, listening.

"My parents, especially my mother was in complete hysterics, but I calmed her down. My colleague was at work. And I called this girl I was casually seeing to leave a message."

"Uh-huh. And?"

"And what? That was it."

"Didn't you call any of your old friends, your high school buddies?"

"Well, I usually speak to them occasionally but not on a routine basis."

"You need to wake up. Open your eyes. Did Chicago not mean anything to you?"

"What? Why? Is it important to drink like you did in college? Is it that important to stay in touch with people from your past? Is it a noble thing?"

"Calm down. There are certain things in life that matter. Jobs, careers, going to college are important. But they don't mean a thing. It's the relationships you build over time, the friends that you make; the love that is true: the love from a stranger. Your parents, your sisters, brothers, cousins, aunts and uncles will always love you."

He stares out the window at the sky. Long pause even for him.

"To find a girl- who loves you- is the key to life, my friend."

"Not all things revolve around love."

"No. You are right, but the most important things do. Yes, your friends are busy. They have a life now that they did not plan. It's the nature of all things that are living and breathing. Trust me, people need people. We are all insecure. Family and *good* friends understand that and accept it."

He drifts off to the window, looking at the sky.

"It's the only thing that matters. I love this state. It is open and free: fields to wonder about, plains to dream upon. Skyscrapers and bright lights are the visions of a shallow man. I have been to Vegas, New York City, LA- I have been in the middle of Mardi Gras. But out here is a world that I understand, a world that makes sense. A world where music in my head plays and nothing around me exists."

I understand clearly this last sentence more than he knows.

"I hear what you're saying. I just can't let go of everything. I have to go back home eventually."

"You can, but trust me. You don't want to deal with the consequences."

He returns to the stare-out-the-window posture.

"Where did you tell your mother you were doing?"

"Just taking a break from everything."

"Did your job call your parent's house?"

I do not respond.

"I know you put them down on your application for an emergency contact. All underachievers do."

He just laughs. I think he finds himself too funny.

"All is a strong word."

"Did you?"

"Yes I did and yes they did."

"Were they wrong to contact your parents?"

"No but... ahh, you're just trying to prove something."

"If you are just figuring that out then we might have to turn around and drop you off at your place."

I take the stare-out-the-window posture.

"Doesn't matter. Won't have it in two weeks."

"Hmm."

"Anyway- why Denver?"

"Why not?"

"C'mon, I've welcomed all these little bits and pieces here and there, the least you can do is tell me why. I went to Chicago to see some of your old friends puke, you puke, I mean, I am patient but give a guy a break here? I'm about to lose everything I worked for."

He finally breaks his look to look at me.

"Your actions define you. By you joining me you have defined yourself."

I have no response to him. My deflation resonates in my voice.

"I just thought this would be fun. A wild time."

"Who's to say it's not? You are an educated person, I can tell by your words and by your stance, posture, and such. But not all things can be bought, given, caught, not even luck. You have to achieve, and achievement takes steps."

He reaches into his console and pushes a button for music.

"This might add some levity."

The divider goes down.

"Hey, Monyak!"

"What's up?"

"Put on the theme song of Superman!"

Suddenly, the music begins, the windows go down and everything I was negatively thinking goes out the window. This is what I needed at this god forsaken point. I sit back, close my eyes and enjoy the music. He must have been watching my facial reactions, because once I forgot about life and smiled, he hit pause and the music stopped.

"That's life. Just when you think everything is in tune, it happens. It's a barricade by design. Do you turn around and go back or do you try to break through the obstacle?"

"Put that shit back on!"

"I must admit, you are probably more intelligent than I am. But right now, you are a student. Does that make you angry? I don't care. You must accept that there is nothing wrong with being a student. In time, you will be a teacher, just not right now."

I flap my arms up in frustration, shake my head. The idiot just stares at the corn.

"You saw my childhood home, the window on the top floor. When I was ten, just a kid, I would stare out the window for hours. The night, the stars, the moon! I would stare beyond the fields, beyond the Great Lakes, beyond the Allegany Mountains, beyond the ocean. I would see a place where everything I ever imagined could come true."

"I'm asking nicely. Could you please restart the song? I have enough problems, recurrences- I don't need this."

"Recurrences? You've been to a therapist?"

"Yes!"

He reaches for the ice, but decides to apt for straight whiskey.

"God, it's hard to find this place. So hard to find Utopia when you grow up and live in America."

"What are you talking about?"

I sit there, staring out at the corn fields. It seems like days, weeks, months and years have gone by. I start the spin of a dream within a dream. I can't stand the vigor my mind takes: what am I doing here? What am I doing with my life? Are my jeans stained? Where is my phone? I need food. Did he accomplish his dreams? Am I just a tool to his madness? Am I to be murdered in nowhere? I calm down for a minute... did his moment pass him by?

"Look- I found you laying on my yard so I will tell you what I know. Philosophy is what you think."

He laughs with a distinct irony to his accusation.

"Parmenides, Aristotle, Plato, Marcus Aurelius, Aquinas, David Hume, Immanuel Kant, Karl Marx and Nietzsche – you know that whole Superman thing? They all had something to offer. They all saw the world from a different perspective. They had a reason to write. My friend, so do I: my philosophy is simple:

"Reality is what you make of it.
Honesty comes within.
Dreams are nothing until they happen.
Memories do not exist unless they are made.
Happiness is a state of mind.
Hope is wishful thinking.
Faith is a reason to live.
Glory– it can only be achieved.
Words– they are defined by action.
Life is simply beautiful.
Death: be not afraid.
Heroes are not found in sports.
Games are what people play.
America is a drug.
People want it, but have to suffer because of it.
Religion is a personal relationship.
It's a challenge to overcome being conquered by years of
    suffering.
Hatred is a form of jealousy.
Authority should be reflected by a mirror.
Love is finding something- no, I mean, anything beautiful.
Christ: He died for mankind.
Think inside the box and make it simple.
Lose one-self and learn something worthwhile to teach."

"This is fine and dandy but what age-old ritual is this?"
He doesn't even acknowledge I am here. TC goes into a
possessed state.

"ONE LIFE, period.
If you like someone then tell them.
If you want to leave then leave!
If you hate your job then quit.

This is the afterlife.
One comes from somewhere.
-The new life is waiting to happen.

God knows the truth.
Question nothing.
Believe me: Socrates did not have the answer.
The three keys to finding a purpose:
1.) Lie, be still and listen to the silence in a dark and empty room.
2.) Walk in a cemetery and take notice to the names.
3.) Write.

He holds up his thumb and two fingers. I am too agitated to ponder these thoughts or think. He believes he is a great philosopher? He has the meaning of life? Does he believe that? He stares at me and laughs like I have my thoughts scrolling across my forehead.

"Okay, fine asshole. I am in a car going to God knows where, probably hell. I have the Fates That Be playing xylophone on my brain with their echoing notes, echoing in my head as we speak. I don't have the friendships that you have, I don't have the life that you lived, I don't have the love you display for some woman I have never seen, I don't have whatever it is that you are trying to achieve. What I do have is a normal life, a normal routine where I can go to work, give in my two-dollar ideas, show up in my ironed two-dollar outfit and be happy. I was happy to punch in and punch out for my satisfaction of a good's day work."

"I can tell you have that persona. You want to be a writer. This is important: see the scene and create the scene. Close your eyes and picture everything in the room: people's action, the reaction, the overall demeanor, the mood of each character. What does the place smell like: is it musty, cloudy or fresh? Think about a women and the way she smells. It's not about the fragrance she wears; it's about her natural scent. I saw Allie once; it was fifteen years later- in a café. We said hello and that was it. That was it... we both knew."

"Can you just put the song back on- I'm sorry, man!"

He takes a long pause to look at the darkness of the clouds approaching. My heart races inside of my chest like a spider spinning its prey before it is sucked dry of blood.

"Sorry, I'm lost in thought. Just capture every little moment in every scene and you will become a great writer."

"Whoever said I wanted to be a writer? I fell in your yard!"

TC hits down the divider and tells Monyak to pull the car over. His demeanor is not good; I know he thinks he is doing me the favor. I look out the window and see no one in sight. This place is like being in an episode of 'The Twilight Zone': barren, desolate, gathering darkness. He grabs something out of the trunk, exits the car and yells to Monyak to reach in the glove box and grab the envelope titled 'Passion'. Monyak hands me the envelope and closes the divider. I look out the window and see TC walking in the field. The crazy thing in my head is that this dude knows exactly where to stop. We're about to cross another state line. I open the envelope and read a large hand-written note above it:

THIS IS MEANT TO BE SUNG BY A MAN AND A WOMAN.

I turn over the notebook paper and read:

PASSION

(<u>MAN</u>)
I don't know
Who I am
-Anymore

I don't know
Where I am

-Anymore

I don't know
Where I'm going
-Anymore

(<u>WOMAN</u>)
Christopher

FEEL
The heartbeat
-It keeps you alive

SEE
The light
-It guides you home

HEAR
The silence
-The insight
-The insight into your soul

(<u>MAN</u>)
Moments and memories
Fade from my thoughts
Sand and time
Slip through my fingers

I BLEED
Passion

I BLEED
Pain

THIS HUNGER
-Inside me
-Yearns

For something
I am not
-Anymore

(<u>WOMAN</u>)
Christopher

TOUCH

The hands
-Can build
A future

Christopher

STARE

The eyes
-Can seek
The truth

Christopher

LISTEN

The music
-Can set
You free

IT'S PASSION

It's why – its why
I believe.

I am so pissed I have to read it again...

And I do. I look around for my smokes and find the pack of Marlboro Reds. I search in the leather seats, in all the compartments, underneath pillows. I can't find my lighter. I look through the window and see him torching my brand new Michigan sweatshirt. I laugh to myself and think this guy doesn't fuck around. Talk about passion. He gets back in the Lincoln.

"What the fuck, I just bought that."

"No, I bought that."

He opens a compartment and grabs a suitcase. He just laughs as he throws on an Ohio State sweatshirt. I will admit it is kind of funny, but I am still pissed off. I have an idea why I'm here. Karma is collecting a loan on me.

"Okay, we might have some weird arrangement, seeing that I fell on your lawn, but the drinking, the emotional roller-coaster with pre-cautions do not give you the right to peer pressure me into the rites of human smuggling for the arts. I know I am here on a whim without the strategic advice of others, and I haven't taken action on my own life, but the dreams I'm starting to have again are causing my manic-depressive state to re-awaken, to collide with the inquiry of why? I don't have the answer; I only have the life to give shape toward my physical, social pathologies of drinking and smoking. This is so not tantamount of my suffering for a solution, because the trauma you create, you gather, you harvest, you collect, support, build, improve, control, or maintain, will not add to the heavy mass upon my heart. I live with the available energy to me, looking to art to change life, not investigate through its remnants. My dreams of having sex and building churches have no meaning to what a human being is- but I should know this! You are nothing but a thought in my head and I noisily and affirmatively accept this. Do I reach boredom? Yes! Like a Russian worker finding art in his work, boredom is our routine and nothing speaks more frankly than a woman in black. This fear, risk, hope: they are the three things I deal with on a daily basis. If everybody understood what you said, what I said, then no one would care or even think. They would listen but not question."

I sit there breathing heavily.

"You're weird."

He leans into the Lincoln, hits down the divider.

"Monyak, shine the lights on the sign."

TC gets out and walks over to the 'WELCOME TO COLORADO' sign. He grabs the tin of Kodiak out of his pocket, stares at the sign and throws in a dip. He walks back and gets in the car.

"Destination, Denver."

He closes the divider and smirks at me.

"You don't want to go home, not yet."

I smile out of my own hilarity. I relax my guard and jump in.

"You have no idea. I love this song."

He hits play on the CD player and the Superman theme song begins at the beginning. As the mountains grow larger I feel I can clear them in a single bound.

CHAPTER **17**

ALTITUDE EFFECT

I assume the suggestion of staying in a hotel room as the proper route to enjoy the splendor of downtown Denver; however, my concession in the benefits was not specific enough to him. Now how was I to persuade him to pay? As we lace around the mountains for this rendezvous, I continue remembering what has transpired the last twelve hours. And it comes in bolts. Lightning bolts. Doomsday: here and presently now, before his replacement of reality and including the after with the unreality of his poems- I cannot reach far enough to what he aspires in accomplishing, because I don't reach far enough, but I dare think I can in this brittle air. And I think about Virginia Woolf, the writer. I enjoyed her consciousness upon life-altering events: marriage, betrayal, murder; but it was a canting, maybe a referendum, of her human character changing in a tangible moment within in her brief history of time. Supposedly our human character can change as consequential as a light switch. And I agree. And if she was supposedly able to place humanity's change of character to a date in the 20th century, than I don't have a time for me but I have a city when it might have altered, for me: it was Denver, September. The details tease any rationale since the events are make-shift, confusing at least.

The rain was healing and annoying this morning, such as my memories and anxiety. Living under vague and elusive labels like fortunate and lucky: who wants to deal with deep, ethical, demanding choices when we only plead for a release or for the volume lowered? Everything is the same but I believe that this sameness echoes a different crunch every time it's brought to the check-out lane of contemplation; the act keeps the thought fluid, buoyant and spatially cleansing. These labels in satiating our dizzying mindfulness for others, whom explicitly see us, receive us, judge us, and/or befriend us, without empathy, is our own peril. It's that damn W.I.I.F.M. question: what's-in-it-for-me?

This pontificating disharmony conducting in my head needs to be wiped clean. This morning walk with the loyal sounds of nature will not skimp on me, and I engage Denver before I lose the all-encompassing ingredient gluing my presence together: curiosity. The curiosity, in over-drive, delves into image, memories, what-if's, of my high school girl compared to his high school girl... I could've done something more? The ping I send out returns, re-surfaces to irritate myself with these random thoughts but I'm afraid if I don't hold the levee then I won't wade into that pool of excessive reassurance: eyelids heavy, thoughts mashed, not a symphony, but noise- the by-products of this process.
"All the time, it gets late."

By saying it out-loud, it's therapeutic. I had to say it out loud so the crying crickets, with their tight and agonized shrills, can hear and TC won't know where I wander. Leave his thoughts in the hotel room while mine hold all the water I can with my cracked glass of demand for attention, eventually holding nothing when I look for an epiphany. In high school, as the ugly introvert, not physically nor internally, insofar as to be unattractive, but ugly by organization and clarity, I never imagined it would be easier to read and fly than question everything but accept just as much.

Is TC too brittle to bring forth the best in me? Can his words withstand the thunder clap and slanting rain of criticism and ignorance and short-sightedness? His intention of sharing is defining in some plan, but my mind has to criminally upset the process with the vision of Steph: the free, light, and white angel that cascaded the dark of 'The Shack' as we briefly visited to re-stock the Lincoln. People around her were lonely, alone, working or drinking, laughing or listening, cool or nervous, deciphering their vicious want for acceptance by her... not me. I felt a connection... I shake my head vigorously, Etch-a-Sketch style: clean the slate.

The rain lets up. Churning with people, hectic and propulsive, the city of Denver slowly took its time from railroad junction and winning dirtiest air quality in the 80's to the envy of many interstate citizens now: these needless nuggets buried and oddly retrievable from hours of bar trivia and Jeopardy. My life's boredom is satisfied this way. Disappointing, maybe, but should I logically end this pattern or envision an otherworldly superiority because of this fighting, grand place? The hilarious outrage and senility in our bourgeoisie life, bounded around the seven deadly sins as virtuous practice, directs me to the Denver library for solace: a book sale is happening. TC didn't come; he sleeps with the bedspread over his head, now and throughout the previous night. If he is dead... damn, I can't think like that. I'm split if I would miss him or be relieved to go home. Figures the fence-walking is in Denver- I'm halfway in all directions.

I enter the library and breathe deeply. I also feel challenged, calm, welcome. I just peruse and let myself wander:

H.G. Wells, Bauhaus designer Laszlo Moholy-Nagy, calling for a Utopian of genius to imagine and build for a future artist. T.S. Eliot considers April as the cruelest month;

his most hated is most peoples' favorite. I find spring is not bad. Wassily Kandinsky warned that Christ said 'the rest you cannot grasp today'. I feel that my wanderings will never be catalogued as logistically as the library's tomes can be. Especially my wanderings at my local water-hole, the Blue Moose in North Royalton, where simple notes meant nothing much except more space on my hard drive, voiceless and unheard. But the people and the energy helps the pen to napkin, so... Oscar Wilde and his writing 'Salome', with his unashamed sensuality versus religious chastity, placed so carelessly next to the latest photo of the Jonas Brothers on People, the Strauss', Richard and Johann, back in the 1800 and 1900, a curious thought- is it too late for repentance in leadership? We could be the most intelligent person or people but would we question, and then interrogate the proper industries to answer for better leadership? I would answer, 'Be Bold, Ask Everything'. I go to the second floor of the library.

I venture across the philosophy section. Struggles to pettiness: is it right? Should wrong be the way of life so when wrong is right you are not disappointed, elated or calm when it happens? As it will be! The pen of thoughts, questions can run dry! To conjure up unwittingly a vision within our one-self: the ultimate deceit and vehement sin! That you are great, unique, different, loving and intelligent- how do you explain the mistake to yourself? The ubiquitous comment 'See you later' by random people meaning I don't give a damn if we see each other again... I need water. Where's the stupid water fountain here?... Finally!

The bookshelves are endless, stirring my mind to wax on more randomness of becoming too pathetic, tight with envy, graded by the negative, corroded from media and money, to a point of being nameless and unrecognizable. I shake out of my day's replay.

Now I stand hollowly, along with the rest of the fellow hotel guests, standing outside due to a lesson implemented by TC: he pulled the fire alarm; he had to. The odds of a fire alarm ringing in the night are too slim, even for me. But what disturbed him to do such a thing? Maybe it was the art installation forum on an artist by the name of Damien? I think back to passing by the glass-front, showcasing a few pieces of his work. One was a VW beetle surgically deconstructed and suspended as a technical drawing, or his other piece of oil barrels dynamically balanced to spin concentrically on their circumferences as the platform rotates, or the classified corn on the cob, each kernel with a telephone prefix: these were all spatially mesmerizing for myself; however, the fervor inside TC was of confusion since it was showing on the outside. I give him a few minutes before I intrude.

"Not satisfied?"

"The pieces are fine: using space and void, becoming occupied by junk. I don't know. Who am I to judge? I am not God."

The pause says more.

"And?"

"Well, art is art, and good art is ambiguous. One person can not judge how another person may be affected by a piece of art. To do so would be ludicrous."

"Are you trying to slide poetry in here for an example of amicable art?"

"Poetry is a window to the soul. Burning down a house is an indication of being fluid, dynamic, forceful, versus working nine to five in the permanent, stagnant and rigid; there is this surrender of the heart that a person must own before liberty is reached. And I feel words and visual images complemented with music have the aggressive, biting acknowledgment... but with tenderness."

He just shakes his head and continues.

"What I just said was not intelligent. It is not who I am. I just want you to figure out who you are, realize that you have potential. Art is sadness and never recognized in its time."

"Nice try, but art can also be confidence exhibiting a sign of power and prosperity."

"Until it collapses into rubble. Edgar Allen Poe wrote in basements. He died broke and ended up in a gutter. You have no idea what it is like living in an attic, creating 'Starry Night.' You have no idea what it is like walking the streets of Europe and being chastised and beaten down like a bum, to have your own nephew in your own house consider you insane. Beethoven understood his purpose. One day, you will hear the music, see the art. One day, you will understand."

"Are you saying you do?"

"No. But I know what it takes to write a masterpiece. A single piece of paper and a pen can change the world. What you write today might be considered garbage, tomorrow brilliant. Great works of art live in the shadows of attics and basements. You my friend are too confident. Your optimism will fall to the side as weeds infiltrate and choke the fruits of your labor, life, and love."

"I argue. Your rootless life and my accompaniment leave us with no home, no significant other, no place to rest without concern for the next minute."

"You don't listen. Why? Trust me kid, just listen to that voice within."

"Stop o' mystic one."

TC leads the walk toward bustling activity in the city's center. I laugh out loud.

"Do you talk like this to everyone? I can understand some of the stereotypes attached to old hermits who write, but, really?"

He turns around to share the laugh.

"You like testing my ability, throwing checkers on a chess board." He turns from me and continues his stride. "I know your mind, the way you think. One day you'll learn that intelligence is a gift. Never fake it."

The clear night gladly offers a cold wind. At least I have normal clothes on. A large majority stand, shaking, in bare essentials, rushed, mismatched, and motley. I still haven't been able to locate TC. Fire engines flash, police walk by, herding people away from the hotel: the tension, aggression from agitation rises. If that wasn't it, what about the bar we went to?

We walk into a bar that swings from comfortable pub to possible club. It was fine to our standards; the only reason we went in was the happen-stance of over-hearing a person on their cell saying they just came from Lava. The time was on the cusp of becoming packed and standing to having prime location with a booth to observe the entire area. We were the latter and the last table available. I hate standing packed tightly with everyone, awkwardly swaying back and forth to accommodate the mob's pulse. Then, she came to our table. Her name was Stephanie, preferring Steph: a petite, porcelain skinned waitress with midnight hair and eyes to match: it was perfect. I glanced to TC and the approval was written all over his face.

"What would you guys like?"

The events were of no dramatic importance from that courtesy opening: TC got a rum and coke, and I a gin and tonic. After being in the car all this time with little to no other scenery, it was all right to simply not talk and watch the environment as if floating above the space, unnoticed and omnipotent to the occupant's interaction. I turned off upstairs in my head and TC was working. Working on what was the mystery. And as I trickled into random thoughts, I conscientiously withdrew, knowing the morning library was enough time worked. With a band warming up, conversation with the bar muse was to flip. I had a vapor of an idea to ask her to come along. And tried to play out how it would sound... and quickly tossed it aside. On our third round, he must have been thinking too much that the words had no where else to go but speak.

"Steph! Ever want to get away. You know, go after your dream?"

She was busy but did not display it. She took a slight pause with her eyes to the ceiling and responded.

"Of course. I'm a writer trying to get enrolled in a creative writing course, UCLA."

TC leans back in the booth; Steph leaves for her other tables.

"Let's ask her along."

I choke on my drink.

"You think we're some caravan, driving cross-country picking up people who have nothing, nothing but a dream? You've gotta be cracked."

"You don't get it. Some day you will."

Her next trip to the table sparked some intrigue because she flicked her hand for me to move over. She sat down; she smelled divine.

"It's funny you asked me because I was thinking about leaving Denver, maybe go back to Minnesota where I'm from."

A simple answer that many people might say was open to a line of dialogue. The problem, I think, was the adamant approach of TC to push her into agreement that her time mustn't be wasted. Back and forth, back and forth, until the inevitable halt by her which would or could undeniably never be construed as agitated. She's got such beauty.

"Should I cut him off?"

Lost in her face, absorbing as fast I could, I stumbled forward with nonsense.

"Well, I mean, look at him, he's gotta be well over fifty."

She gets up and the visits weren't as frequent. I receive a wet stirrer in my face from him.

"Boy, you are smooth, but not that smooth."

"You're no spring chicken yourself."

"Yeah, I know."

"Let me just go on a limb here and recap: have her pack a bag, if that, and jump in a Lincoln with two male strangers... Yeah, that is smooth."

"Yeah, why not?"

With a wave of the hand I blow him off because I have nothing to retort except stammers and but's. This could have happened if we were back in the fifty's, the sixty's. But the post-modern period has eroded to malicious, depraved violence. And so did the rest of the time. Drunken tom-foolery from others, a couple of more drinks, innocent and satisfying flirting, and a good-bye to Steph, stilted and sudden, a night spent to never have again with nothing to show for it. That's probably what made him so agitated. It was her answers to TC's probing interest that almost sold her. From oddities to blunt stubbornness, her responses were talented but mismanaged:

"A memoir of a privileged life erroneously wasted when I sleep... that's what I want to write. Under the Big Sky of Montana."

"To live without provoking the devils when investing benevolence in angels' words."

"You guys sound fantastic but, seriously, who's gonna believe that?"

"Passion is great to have. It helps you from the coveting nature we share our land and lives with people as meaningful as a song title."

"Here's my email address. I'll send you the first draft when I get accepted into that course and be brutally honest with me."

I imagined in my head what her voice would have been if she said:

"You know what? I will! I get off at 1am. Pick me up then!"

But she didn't, she wouldn't; it's a shame but I can't fault her. The walk back must have occupied his mind as her face and mannerisms did mine.

I decide to go looking for TC through the mob outside the hotel since the desire of finding why he did such a thing. The wintry disdain of the people was growing hostile. To put all the people out in the night, from their sleep, to watch, to observe and view; felicity of their dreams turned into brooding hate, hate carrying over to the staff, families, peers, friends...

The fire engines and police cars continue with their whine and lights outside the hotel. The people bustle like scared cattle. I start believing this lesson was a chance for the stranded people to learn perspective but not for all to get. These people have their own worlds to spin on, to rotate on their own axial agendas, not ours. But if they learned against the fatigue and lack of care as a surplus in their mind to bank, then they might agree and understand! Do you know how many deaths we all have died to be re-birthed and re-taught? You will never regain the secret you once had, that elated, joyous laughing, once heard from our innocent child's mouth and imagination.

Flat, numb, disconsolate, bored, expression-less: never cooperate, always compete. Walking in this sea of people and noise leads me to want coffee; everybody else would prefer sleep. I wish simplicity could be easier. It is sensible, rational, and realistic. My yearning is wrought from episodes of naïve idealism in masculinity, no weak femininity allowed here. I am man: I want, I get. I find him waving me in a side door. I walk through the hotel, going back to the room, as TC drone on like the anthropomorphic villain, HAL. I'd prefer to sit in the room, alone, listening to a symphony over and over from my favorite concerto. I'm still undecided: was it the exhibit, was it not asking Steph to join, what could the two hour fire drill really teach. Maybe he wanted to catch people at their most susceptible. I find the lesson an example of the fallacy in existence. The bait and switch of happiness directly related to the number of achievements and recognition collected. I want to say something but I feel as a blind man judged on my ability to play baseball. Will I have enough time to integrate my life with all the data and the options and the potential effort I have in front of me? What if all my dark, licentious desires embarrass me and I never reach the outlet to convert this rawness into intelligent, professional rewards? Will I be spent searching for the corner in a circular room? Will the sandcastles of TC's life be there after forty nights of rain?

It could be my fault to innovate upon the brain, no less, an excuse, or disclaimer, lying in this room, this linchpin, teetering in the middle of the country; but I have to keep interrogating the cosmos. My mind doesn't give up easily and shifts over to Freud's sexual knowledge in images and repression. But then I come across the futility of language and how airplanes may be the answer since it is technology, tech, to get us into space, to worm-holes and sleek, stylish pods where we can have cool silence and the eponymous sliding door noise from the film, 'Star Wars'... or maybe I can stay behind on the earth and figure a way to recreate

Duchamp's genius in marketing a ball of twine with a hidden noise, or, simply, marketing a toilet. Modern language is supposed to speak of intelligence but I find modern language actually unknown to its benefactor and the individual's beneficiaries.

The silence in the hotel room keeps fueling my inner-minded predictability. As custodian of this jaunt in high school hi-jinks and ulterior possibilities, will I have the chance for a no do-over? If I keep answering myself with the same thing, same answer, to an ever-changing test question, would I eventually be right? Right? Right. A raw, untamed noise ruins my rapacious libido for continuing, my penitentiary of the mind keeps the lights always on. How quickly we got here though: before it was clouds of steam gushing from manholes in Chicago now replaced with hot springs and steam gliding over spas in the Snow Mountains of Denver. The oxygen here is messing with my under-stimulated brain and gaunt appetite for sleep. My walking in Denver will be replaced with walking Las Vegas as the human wheels of legs will immerse myself in a varying stigma of predestined losers or impoverished lower class; its these vile, disgusting labels conjured by people whom spew muck, needles and used condoms into the forest of my internal self with strange endemic results. To lose our solemn vow in sustaining ambivalence toward ambition from these images; I do not. I do not trash the broken promises and lost friendships because reality is a commodity... but human. I wish I was going back to the exhibit through downtown Denver with its clean, superlative surroundings; we were probably the dirtiest things in that four block quad in the Art District, but me, and TC will blend in Vegas. And If I'm right, the road will take us there. And right now, I need to stop thinking like this. These over-stuffed words have to be accelerating the loss of space for the few memories that I cherish. Then, the silence is broken as he tells me something I didn't expect.

"Just for the record... I didn't pull the alarm."

CHAPTER 18

PARALLELS OF LIFE ARE WASTED

Exiting Denver in the night was a quiet time. There was not much talking; I'm glad for it, because I remember a time, not too far back, creating another chore from happen-stance of asking. The corollary can exist if I force it, but whoever said the fragments couldn't make a half drawn picture where I can automatically fill in the gaps? But isn't that the point? Filling in the gaps where misunderstanding exists? I watch the passing landscape of sheer mountain faces, hair-pin curves, and an eighty-foot distance from the left side of the Lincoln equating to a fiery ball.   I-70 West, the Rocky Mountains, the Eisenhower tunnel, the Colorado River, the fresh air; pure oxygen makes it all alive, all beautiful, the red mountains lit up by the rising sun, a black hawk gliding overhead. I float by myself for a while.

Nevada is barren: a dry land of cactus and tumbleweed. My mouth is being filled with cotton while my skin sweats off the humidity. Vultures hover above the road kill. I close my eyes with vultures' careful eye on me, boring into me... Monyak interrupts my zone. He must be in a hurry. We have to be going about a hundred and fifty miles an hour. What are we late for? There must be a reason. Or a reason? TC loves the speed and the moment. He rolls down the window and lets the wind blow back his hair.

"Think of this."

He looks out at the desert plains and reflects:

"The Rocky Mountains
　　The White Water Canyons
　　　The Scenery.
A City Street
　　　A Woman
　　　A White Dress.
　　Amazing
　　　Truly amazing
The Feeling
　　　The Heartbeat
　　　　The Wind
　　　The Light
　　The Ground
　　　The Death
　　　　The Arrival."

He packs his tin and throws in a dip.

"Can you hear the American Greed, The Machine at its best, kid. Welcome to Las Vegas: where the nostalgic casinos are being replaced by the phantom billionaires of today, the spirit of Sinatra, Martin, Sammy Travis, Bogart and Hepburn is torn apart by bulldozers and cranes while Elvis, the King, is being buried again beneath the rubble."

Monyak slams on the brakes in front of the zoo, the MGM Grand; we enter: TC with a duffel bag; me, I have a clean shirt on with fading deodorant, again. We walk past the suits, the vacationers, the day-trippers, valet attendants, and bellmen. I follow TC to the front desk. An attractive dark-haired woman in her late twenties stands behind the counter: this isn't Burger King.

"My good friend, Monyak, made a reservation for the Hollywood Suite."

The woman tickles her computer for a bit, looks around and bites her bottom lip.

"Let me guess, the room is not available?"

"Well, sir. The reservation, I mean check-in, was an hour ago."

"What's the difference? MGM saves some money by me arriving late."

"I'm sorry sir, but a sheik from Saudi Arabia wanted the room. He pays three times the amount for everything."

TC laughs. He never had a suite lined up.

"You know what, no big deal. Just give me any room."

She leaves, noticeably unphased and uses a computer at another station. TC looks at me and shakes his head.

"I should have worn an Armani Suit and held a briefcase filled with yesterday's stock prices."

I am stupid to ask, but I do-

"Why?"

"Deceit in this world, especially here, is everything. That's why."

The woman returns with two card keys.

"These keys will work in an hour, sixteenth floor, room 23. We'll comp the breakfast buffet for you."

"No, don't, just have a twelve pack of Budweiser on ice in the sink."

"Sir, we ca-"

"Yes, you can. Here is two hundred dollars for making you feel embarrassed. Thank you... Joanne."

I follow TC into the casino and into a lounge. He could've waited at least to hear her deny him again but I just want to get to the floor. But then... the world of a casino floor mesmerizes me.

I decide to flip my attention to what's around me. A petite girl, a modest twenty-three years of age, carries a tray of drinks. Her facial expression of pure jubilee emits freely. She navigates throughout the universe of flashing lights, the mass amalgamation from acute chirps, cacophonous symphonies of coins falling, the generic music, the opalescent smoke trails to the decadent debauchery of greed, adultery, and shameless routines for luck do not distract her. Her poise is impeccable and worth noting since she is serving cocktails that actually have liquor in them, considering a casino's tight control.

"Gin and tonic and a Cuba Libre. Thanks Kiki."

Her smile can melt an iceberg. I sit back in the lounge chair nested on a level that oversees the relevant playing field. I can now sit casually knowing we have a room and a place to stay for the night, that a shower and a change of clothes is in my future. Hell, maybe a rolling jackpot. A nice blazer might make the time worthwhile. Being here is the surreal meal I needed to nourish and fight the toxic entity of self-doubt. I watch, absorb, wonder, and ponder in the simplest of effort. However, the strength of winning a lifestyle dressed in such flamboyance, hitting the big jackpot, doubling down for blackjack, betting everything on red, has always enticed me with such grandiosity that it shames me to speak of the extremities.

"Don't get too comfortable, kid. It's just a playground."

TC takes his seat with a similar angle out to the main lobby. I see Kiki serving drinks to another couple with the same electricity in her smile. Damn.

"Our business is short here so make the most of it."

"I plan on it. So this jaunt to Las Vegas is what? Gamble away your nest egg? Conquer the tables of poker and end up on the local news for collecting the largest jackpot?"

"Don't be a moron. How much money do you have?"

"I pulled forty dollars out of the ATM."

"Total?"

"Why? What do you have?"

"I have access to about a hundred and eighty dollars."

"That's it?"

"C'mon, total."

"Umm, I guess... maybe a hundred sixty, a hundred fifty."

"Hmm, might be trouble. Hang tight."

TC jumps from his chair and disappears easily in the masses. The scenario and scenery flips to a growing pain inside my gut. I continue on the harrowing, splintered images of my buffoonery. Why did he have to follow me? I was at least humble with reading his stupid poem to the bartender back in Ohio. I take a deep breath to stop the inflation of over-reacting. He probably showed me that picture of the ocean because there's probably a pier I can sleep under. I toyed with the thought as a preposterous joke to my parents, but now, sitting here, I foreshadowed my destiny. Fucking old man. Where's Kiki? TC returns.

"Okay, we got some time. I'll get next round.... Why so glum, Pumpkin?"

"Who are you?"

"Calm down and wait for your next drink. We got about... an hour to kill. Besides, this envelope will get you some more money."

He plops a business sized hotel envelope on the table. I reach for it. He snatches it back.

"Not yet."

TC scans the floor with agile ease.

"Well if you're calm, then I am."

"Who said I am? I'm terrified. A hundred fifty, possibly a hundred sixty, I don't know."

I slam my hand on the table.

"C'mon! What is that shit?!"

His shitty grin comes back. He shakes his head at my gullibility.

"Why do you keep scanning the floor?"

Kiki returns: all is grand for the minute.

"I'll take a bottled water, a beer, you pick it, and Junior will have another Gin n Tonic."

She giggles: majestic. She leaves: back to stupidity and stupid.

"C'mon tiger, relax. We have a brief night so use it to collect your thoughts."

"What thoughts? Insanity? You bring me out to Vegas, ask for all my money, tell me it's not enough, and point to this white envelope saying this will make us more."

He looks up in a sarcastic ponder. I focus on the people who are having fun, gambling, people who have money, who come out with their friends, having fun.

"Ask me a question."

I push the glass to the edge of the table.

"What's in the envelope?"

"Can't tell you."

"Okay, what are we doing here?"

"Can't tell you that. Pick something else."

Flustered, frustrated I sit. At least I have Kiki for one more visit. I'm starting to get tired of repeating how I got here.

"Give me a second."

I don't bother coming up with another question. I embrace the presence of all sounds showering upon my aluminum, makeshift status that could fall with the slightest gust or downpour. My thoughts are getting the best of me. I take my cell phone out of my pocket and foolishly forget the time difference. Or the harrowing thought that I really have no one to call. Where is Kiki anyway?

The hour is up and I follow behind him with a stronger posture. I am surprised how good that hour did for me. TC stops at a crossroads on the casino floor: slots, keno, straight ahead; craps to the left and the card tables to the right. Standing here, waiting for instructions from him, I find the location humming with a synergy, as if this was the crux of electricity powering the building and the people.

"Here is the envelope. What I want you to do is give this envelope to anyone of these people gambling. I have to take care of something. Make sure you are at the west side of the casino in 15 minutes."

His stare was so possessed I swear I saw his pupils vibrate. I didn't say a word. I grabbed the envelope and instantly went to task completely missing which direction he went. I stand stoic; legs pinned to the floor, slowly absorbing the mysterious energy underneath the floor, slowly perusing the myriad amount of candidates. The oddity was the utmost confidence I exuded as if this was my full time job. My scan is interrupted by a crash of coins. A woman crumbles to the floor, shirt un-tucked, hair uncombed, scavenging for her coins from the floor like she hasn't ate in days. I open the envelope, pull a worn piece of paper and read.

15

To see a star
And to use that star
To guide you home

To hit a chord
And to strike that chord
Within somebody

To hear a voice
And to use that voice
To be someone

To watch a moment
And to use that moment

To make a movie

To read a book
And to use that book
To change your life

To have a thought
And to use that thought
To make a difference

To feel the ocean
And to use that ocean
To make it happen

To take a step
And to use that step
To launch into the light

{Piano solo}

To be honest
And to use honesty
To better mankind

To have hope
And to use hope
To not be judgmental

To find peace
And to discover peace
To quiet your soul

To understand love
And to use love
To help change this world

To discover faith

And to use faith
To be closer to God

Believe
Dream
-One life
--One life
---One life.

I grasp the writing as being systematic like Mozart, yet passionate like Beethoven; I ponder on the title. Peculiar as it is, nonetheless, eclectic and imperceptibly poignant. My mind imagines his words dancing a waltz with this woman I feel empathy for; I begin my approach. As I get closer, her appearance is worse than originally thought. Maybe she hasn't eaten in days. I'm two steps away with no idea of what I will say. One step away: we need money.

"Ma'am, here's a poem that was written specifically for you."

I hand her the poem and she reads.

"What the fuck is this?"

She throws it in my face and walks away. I look to see TC laughing in the corner. This man laughs a lot but, this time, I can tell he's not laughing at me: he's laughing at the woman's ignorance. Are people so self-centered that not even a poem can warm their icy heart? My head oscillates in deep thought and simple thought. I'm reminded of some of the moments I had back at his home. And I end up on the same redundancy: who is this guy? Is he somebody famous?

He waves me to the elevator and we exit on the sixteenth-floor making our way around as a clumsy tourist. A husband and wife unabashedly complain about the money he has gambled away. Who knows if it was their house, their next car, possibly their children's college fund, perhaps their future together? We enter room 23 and in the bathroom is what he asked for: a sink filled with ice and Budweiser. TC takes out two beers and scans the room. He grabs the desk light and places it in the corner near the window looking out at another casino. The amount of activity from the lit squares is truly curious. You could spend all night just watching from your window and observe people doing their private things from a public venue... but too creepy for me to participate. I know what happened to Jimmy Stewart. TC grabs a notepad and a pen and throws himself into the small lounge chair, cracking a beer open and smiling in this exact moment, silent. I'm bothered.

"What the hell are you doing? We're in Vegas, man. Let's go back down."

"Fuck Vegas. There's an envelope in the front pocket of my bag."

I unzip the bag and find an envelope. It's titled: A Hundred American Chances.

I should be happy, but for some reason I feel cheated. I place the twenties in my wallet.

"Hey kid, I know Vegas. I know money. I know how much I gave you. Think of this, you have thirty kids in a class, nowadays two hundred. It doesn't matter, you give a girl a dollar and she's happy, then you give the boy next to her ten dollars. The dollar was free and she was ecstatic, until the moment the boy next to her got ten dollars."

I ponder on it but his train of thought falls short for me.

"The hell you talking about?"

"Exactly, but it happens every day."

I walk away shaking my head.

"Don't bet it all on #23."

"Why?"

"Because #23 will either beat you or help you win."

I open the door and try to leave.

"Remember where you're from."

I feel like slamming the door, but subconsciously know better and close the door: another time in Las Vegas... alone again.

I walk through the casino slowly observing all the small details: how a fellow gambling man prepares for his big roll, how an elderly lady perpetually chain-smokes with an oxygen tank next to her, playing three slots at once, leashed to one with her rewards card, how women in expansive, red-carpet caliber dress, scan the floor; how the average gambler on a prepared trip shrewdly pick and choose their perfect slot machine, seeing this one but at the last second using the one next to it. The details fade into categories that really don't deviate from this. I leave this area.

I walk into the oasis in the desert: the pool area. I locate the bar and think, why not? I order a strawberry daiquiri. Twenty dollars later, a fruit salad in a glass, and me carrying this, catching giggles from the taut, bikini-clad women: I hate it. I can't walk around with this. I move to a patio chair and watch women in bikinis flaunt their TV ad bodies. Are they waiting for a Bud Light semi to bust through the fence? Are they going to jump in the pool and play volleyball as dudes run in with a six thousand dollar smile? The drink is smooth, like the smooth air at this perfectly late summer dusk: the atmosphere is promising. Vegas is that niche: always making the possibilities realistic no matter your situation. I finish the meal of fruit and step onto the strip. I'm instantly handed four different nudie cards promising the best company or massage. Or in previous tales passed to me: robbery. I collect because my nephews could have the upper-hand in trading sport-cards at school. Damn, am I falling into that rut of thought that everyone is evil? I wander around to get back in the casino as thousands of people walk-about. It is truly a sight to see so many people of all dress, ethnicity, and demeanor in one big aquarium in the desert. Humans never fail to amaze. I make it back in the casino and stop at a roulette table, throwing 60 on black. But suddenly grasp it back before the croupier waves the Hand. The little ball rotates around, wandering like the orbits of space. It's all so poignant with this confusing scenario I'm in, thinking in hind-sight, I was in Ohio about a week ago, listlessly sitting on a phone, taking orders for random business products. The ball clanks around and lands on red #23. Figures. So I open the flood-gates of rational thought into gambling. The hurricane of this and that of probability ruins the moment so I play red. It comes up zero. Nice. A man in a baseball cap wins a stack of chips but stays chiseled: no emotion when he gets his payday. Winning isn't enough I guess. Now that most of the money I was given is gone, I lose the sense of all possibilities available, I head back to the table where Kiki was serving. I'm approached by a make-up layered, middle age woman. The outfit has to be her biggest issue with the job: a strapless bustier and a polyester tutu. I order two drinks knowing I'm down to my last twenty. Who knows if I still have the hundred-fifty I think I have.

The drinks arrive and a band begins to play. I sit there and barely listen to the cover songs the female singer tries oh-so hard to copy. The vacuum of being here is turning my head into wasteful complaints. I down the watered booze quick and head back to the room. TC would make this more fun.

I come back to the room to find six empty beer cans and a few empty one shot bottles. TC stands, hunched over the dresser.

"Are you alright?"

"No. Being in a casino, you lose track of time. It might be the time change or the recycled air of losers they pump into this place. The days become nights; the nights become days: I'm not sure. Do you lose wisdom when you reach adulthood or gain back your childhood when you are an old man? Who the fuck knows? Is that why adults love coming to Vegas, to play games again?"

He cracks open another beer. I grab a beer, stand back and listen.

"My Uncle Jim started his bucket list at sixty-five. His three daughters, my cousins: Dawn, Kelly and Bonnie; all great girls, my sisters, Traci and Terri; family. I grew up around five extraordinary women. I would have made a great husband."

He stumbles into the bathroom. I wonder if I have an escalating situation here. The last thing I need is this old man crying. I stand still for a minute but then hear a few noises and then the shower. Good. I'll let him sober up. I walk over to the dresser and read:

INSPIRED BY BOB DYLAN. I STARTED WRITING THIS WHEN I WAS A KID. I FINISH THIS NOW AS AN OLD MAN. ENJOY...

SEQUENCE OF DREAMS

A world within a world
Where fantasy becomes reality
And make believe is something to believe
In dreams
Comes a darkness, this complete blackness
Creates visions, that line up
In sequence

I was running, running out of time
And I was searching, searching for what was mine

182

And I am coming, coming faster by train
Over rough terrain

I am withering, withering down
Gathering, gathering things around
But losing, losing what I found
Without a sound

I was trying, trying to figure it out
Just wanting, wanting to live it out

In a Sequence of Dreams
Nothing is the way it seems
Imagining things
In a Sequence of Dreams

I was falling... In another day
Throwing... This all away
Believing... You would stay
If only... There was a way
To go back... To yesterday
And bring you back... today

In a Sequence of Dreams
Nothing is the way it seems
Imagining things
In a Sequence of Dreams

I saw her coming
This dream of overcoming
My fears
I was drowning
To the top
I was climbing
Reaching
For an opening

Into one
I am out of the other
Going through
In need of another

Beautiful girl

An ocean pearl
This fantasy world
In which I live in

A Sequence of Dreams
Waking me up when she screams
Life is not the way it seems
In a Sequence of Dreams

I was sinking
Or was I staying afloat
In a river
Outside a boat
In need of a coat
Then I can float

To where it is real
Not spinning on a wheel
Imagination
Is it all that I feel?

In a Sequence of Dreams
It is the way it seems
No more imagining things
In a Sequence of Dreams

I am running, running out of time
And I am searching, searching for what is mine
In a past, in a past- that I cannot seem to find
This present, a present to unwind

So unkind
Is this

I found myself
In a Sequence of Dreams
Just living
In a Sequence of Dreams

(Reality is my fantasy And my fantasy is now my reality)

I lay down- the words I just read wrapping themselves around me as he probably pounds his head into the shower wall. My thoughts of everyday life and reality sounds like the end of a Tommy James and the Shondells song, 'Crimson and Clover', but on repeat. I turn on the generic radio and leave whatever station is on. I have no desire to turn on the TV. Even if I did, I can't find the remote. My selfishness arises without a filter of compassion.

"Could you leave a couple of beers?"

With a compilation of unknown noises and where from, three beers roll out to hit the wall, I get up and bring them back to the table. And then... I think otherwise. I take the beers and myself over to the lounge chair looking out to the other hotel with its circuit-board of windows and people doing their own thing and nestle in. I have no choice. So I watch. And I do it against all inherent principles, but I rationalize because they are the ones who left the curtains drawn open, they are the ones who subconsciously know they leave the curtains drawn because they want to be exhibited. So I watch... and I listen to the radio with a three pack of beer, a few bucks in my jeans, TC in the shower, probably dying, and the radio playing songs. And I'm in Vegas and this is what I'm doing... alone again.

Six hours later, I awake in a drunken haze. I hear the shower and I remember TC. I run over and open the door. I move back the shower curtain and find him sitting in the tub in a T-shirt and boxers with a beer still in his hand. I slap his face a few times and he wakes up. TC rubs his hung over head and blood shot eyes.

"What the fuck, give me a minute."

"Well damn, asshole, what the fuck is this?"

I slam the door without concern, walk back to my chair and pick up the remote. I watch some SportsCenter and see the commentators ripping the state of Ohio. I raise the volume. Suddenly, the bathroom door opens with TC running out to listen.

"God, Skip Bayless really hates Ohio State. Did he even play sports?"

TC wears an Ohio State t-shirt and jeans; clean. Wow, it's like a Jekyll and Hyde thing. He looks at me.

"What the fuck, are you ready to go?"

I look out the window and see all the rooms lost from the circuit-board, hidden in curtains.

CHAPTER 19

TO LET GO OF LOVE IS TO LOVE

Again... in the Lincoln: I want to think simple, but so many things, not just in my life, but others, have expired, with many a thought or thoughts laying, in a library, in a tome, unheard and unheralded. I scratch the slate clean because I have to think simple; I roll the window down; the cool night breeze refreshes. I want to sleep and wake up in the bed I never use, or at least, on my couch, but I can't. We pass the sign you hear about– Los Angeles 423 miles. If L.A is the place, I want to argue and I want to question; I do neither.

Unless we're driving to Hawaii.

A smirk slips out from me; I pity myself for chuckling at my last comment. 'A Long December' by Counting Crows, begins to fill the car. A song of immense depth and brevity: the kernels of memories blast into popcorn of images... I'm earnestly sad to hear the song end. TC rolls down the window and yells with the wind.

"IT'S BEAUTIFUL.
I HEAR IT ALL...
THE WIND, THE OCEAN, AND THE CHILDREN– LAUGHING
THE DRUM, THE PIANO, AND THE WOMAN– SINGING

IT'S BEAUTIFUL.
I SEE IT ALL...
THE MOUNTAINS, THE SKY, AND THE RIVER– FLOWING
THE MOON, THE STARS, AND THE SUN– GLOWING

IT'S BEAUTIFUL.
I FEEL IT ALL…
THE TOUCH, THE KISS, AND THE GIRL - --- LOVING
THE HEART, THE MIND, AND THE SOUL- LIVING

MY FRIEND,
I AM ALIVE

IT'S BEAUTIFUL."

He reels back to throw ice in two glasses and pours whisky from the canter. I take the glass he hands me expecting a State of the Union address.

"This sucks. This journey won't last forever."

I have liquor in my hand, Los Angeles on the mind, and the present is more important than the consequences right now. For all the decisions I've made, the learning curve is beginning to taper to a receding, approachable level. My mind is a sponge at this point, just listen, and register his words. Am I learning the reason to open my ears without presuppositions; am I learning to open my eyes and see the beauty in living versus to live? He sniffs his glass, mustering his thoughts as well as the aroma. He smiles, opens his eyes wide, and laughs large.

"Don't get too comfortable. Here. Inside are two poems. They only took about ten minutes to write."

I pause at the hand-out, take a deep breath and reach for the little envelope. I'm no longer naïve in Camelot or in unicorns so I don't look forward to anything anymore but I am this: a reader-

IT'S AMERICA

To see beyond the horizon
To rise before the sunrise
To drive across the country

To see

The lakes and the rivers
The mountains and the sea
The country and the city

IT'S AMERICA

It's Chicago to Colorado
New Orleans to Seattle
Washington D.C to L.A
New York City to Texas

IT'S AMERICA

It's the Cleveland Browns and the Pittsburgh Steelers
It's the Green Bay Packers and the Chicago Bears
It's the Red Sox and the Yankees
Michigan and Ohio State

IT'S AMERICA

It's the girl next door and apple pie
It's a hot summer day and a long camp fire night
It's fishing, drinking, golfing- just loving

IT'S AMERICA

It's the steel worker and the Ford Mustang
It's a cold Budweiser and Paul Newman
It's a race car and a damn good spaghetti sauce

IT'S AMERICA

It's a drive-in theater and a cheeseburger
It's a high school dance and a homecoming queen
It's a bottle of Jack and a good old friend

IT'S AMERICA

It's a brother and a sister
A son and a father
A mother and a daughter
Trying on that DRESS

IT'S AMERICA

It's the American Flag
And it's the soldier

It's the heart
And it's the song

It's the dream
And it's the soul

IT'S AMERICA

I must admit he is clockwork: he leans over and fills my glass. I attempt to respond but he gestures to turn over the page. I read.

ART

ART
A black kid
And a white kid
Shaking hands

ART
An old man
Sitting on a bench
Feeding the birds

ART
A young girl
Alone in a room
Playing a guitar

ART
A young boy
Hitting a homerun
Rounding the bases

ART
A gymnast
With a broken ankle
In the Olympics
(Keri Strug moment)

ART
A tree
Alone
In the Desert

ART
A whale
Emerging
From the sea

ART
A log cabin
In Connecticut
In winter

ART
A jazz club
Late at night
On Bourbon Street

ART
A mountain
And a river
In New York State

ART
A pier
And a sunset
In Malibu

ART
A field
And a farm
In Nebraska

ART
A fort
In the middle of the woods
In the middle of nowhere

ART
A soldier
Holding his best friend
In his arms

ART
Beethoven
Conducting his Ninth Symphony
Michelangelo
Painting the Sistine Chapel

ART

A Mother
And her son
Eating ice cream

ART
A Father
And his daughter
On her wedding day

ART
A friend
And a friend
Fishing… on a lake

ART
A young girl
Lying in bed
With cancer

ART
An old woman
Staring from a window
At Grandchildren

ART
A baseball game

ART
A woman's back
(Kate Hudson –in How to Lose a Guy)
A woman's smile
(Julia Roberts –Pretty Woman)
A woman
(Keira Knightley –Love Actually)

ART
A thought

A prayer (Doves fly)
A hope

ART
A candle
A moment
A life

ART.

I finish and look to TC as if there was another step. He is back to gazing out the window. I want to ponder his words of what is beautiful, to what is America, to what is art. His dependence to these things is unmistakable, but taking this journey across country makes me wonder about his perceivable avoidance of it all... and to live simply. Why would he be casual to the burning down of his house, arrange the quick meeting with friends that I think was prearranged, and the continued barrage of writing that lingers on my brain as unread until the first time by me? I speak to myself in declaration, deliberately scratching these itchy words to bounce loud:

His unfortunate wish may ironically be wishing you were in the company of this beauty, this America, or this art. Are you not surrounded by this dome of co-existing with others to share and to be heard? It leads to question my last memory of sitting at the good-old Blue Moose in Ohio with this Mexican Man and the break-up I was going through. The hurt love, the cracked existence of using cheap paste to replace, the routine beat-down of a job that pressured you more and more into oblivion. Pablo and me, Piet Mondrian, have to leave you now. You have pocket aces don't forget.

TC interrupts with a postcard of the Grand Canyon. Music begins to play softly on the speakers, 'Please Forgive Me' by David Gray. I turn it over and read:

ALLIE,

You are the only person in the world that will ever understand me.
You will always have my heart.
You will always have that little child inside me
 -that stared out the window and saw the stars.
You, Allie -are a part of my dreams.

Forever - I miss you
Teddy

He reacts first.

"I don't mean to sound like such a pussy. I just know what's important. Love, love is the only thing that really matters in life."

He hands me another envelope titled 'The Perfect Day'. I open the envelope; this time unsealed, and unfolds the crisp sheet of paper to read-

THE PERFECT DAY

Forget the convertible Audi ride on the Pacific Coast Highway and dinner at Decks in Malibu, where the Pacific Ocean is outside a huge, picturesque window.

No, what I Imagine for the two of us is this: The day would start off slow at my place: In this cozy little loft in New York City. We would order a pizza and watch a funny movie like 'How to Lose a Guy in Ten Days'. You would sit in my arms with your head lying against my chest. We may wrestle around a little on the couch – Playful wrestling –just fun. We would eat the pizza and watch the end of the movie. I would hand you a tissue B/C the movie would make you cry – oh wait –you would probably hand me a tissue. We would play around – I would pin you and passionately kiss you. Playtime would be over; we would MAKE LOVE on the floor. We would be exhausted... and laugh all naked on the floor –staring at the ceiling because it will have been 15 years. We would eat a few pieces of pizza sitting across from each other, on the floor, against the wall. Then we would make a chocolate mousse pie. (With or Without You just came on as I am writing this – how amazing –our song –our very first time). Back to the perfect day, we would watch a little T.V –you in my arms. The pie would get done and we would be in the kitchen standing by the table – we would share bites until I took the whip cream and spread it all over your face – A food fight would begin. I would be taking the chocolate and throwing it down the white button up shirt of mine you are wearing. Things would turn viciously arousing. We would rip each other's clothes off and lick off the pie then have sex on the table, on the counter and maybe even the stove. Next, we would take a shower, because I have taken more showers with you than probably by myself. The window would be open and we would be able to see the sunset –from the shower. A light yet warm breeze would hit our naked bodies as I from behind you – would wash your legs, chest and feet. Time would stop and I would wash your long dark hair. We would dry off and walk to the bedroom in our towels. I would light a candle and we would have good sex on the dresser. Next, you would be in the room getting dressed –I would be in the kitchen. I would yell. Hey Hun ---You are amazing. You would come out as I was pouring a glass of champagne. Your hair would still be wet. Strawberries would be in a bowl. We would sit across from each other at this little table with high chairs. Eating strawberries and drinking champagne. I would open the window to a warm summer night. The white curtain would gently sway in the wind. I would pour us another glass and say... Come with me –I want to show you something. I would lead you down the stairs and out into the midnight. We would walk to Central Park and sit on the bench. I would place my arm around you and we would watch the stars. We would finish the champagne and leave the glasses on the bench and walk hand in hand back home. We would enter the bedroom and I would tell you... I LOVE YOU... I always have... I always will. You would look into my eyes and say... I have loved you from the first moment I saw you. The moment would be intense... so much passion would be in that room. We would MAKE LOVE on the bed. We would look so deep into one another's eyes and feel the other ones soul. It would end with our two bodies entwined in a mutual orgasm. We would look at each other and SMILE. We would both know that our love could never die. We then would lie naked face to face and talk. Hours would pass by. Then as you were falling asleep –I would say... Allie ----This was the greatest day of my life. I love you. Your eyes would open. You would lean up with a tear in your eye and say... No one ever told me that this kind of love existed. Ted ----I will love you forever. You would fall asleep in my arms and I would fall asleep in your arms and we would never wake up.

Written to Allie - my first love - my high school sweetheart

Ted Christopher
July 1, 2007

I finish reading and he instantly hands me another envelope. This flood of more words is overwhelming but I read with the door open to my unconscious. Is this all a test? Is all this going to make the gestating worry of my consequences disappear? The envelope is titled 'Closure'. The divider goes down, TC motions for Monyak to stop the car; TC gets out of the car, without closing the door. I watch him walk into the desert and lie flat upon his back in the sand. He just lies there and stares at the moon. I open the envelope, unfold the sheet of paper and read.

CLOSURE

To the eyes
That open
But cannot see

To the ears
That hear
But do not listen

To the mind
That wonders
But does not think

To the body
That hurts
But refuses to suffer

MY DARLING
I'M SORRY
I'M SORRY

It was me
A struggle
That was meant to be

To the light
That glows
But cannot burn

To the water
That flows
But does not heal

To the day
That begins
But does not end

To the night
That ends
But cannot begin

MY DARLING
IM SORRY
IM SORRY

It was me
A struggle
That was meant to be

To the spark
That ignites a flame
But burns out

To the hand

That buries a man
That can't survive

MY DARLING
IM SORRY
IM SORRY

It was me
A struggle
That was meant to be

To the soul
That plays
But does not sing

To the heart
That feels
But cannot love

MY DARLING
I'M SORRY
I'M SORRY

It was me
A struggle
That was meant to be

To the girl
That cried

To the boy
That tried

MY DARLING

It's to the dream

That lived

And never died

...GOOD-BYE

I finish with a moment of silence, when 'Goodbye My Lover' by James Blunt begins. I look out the open door and see TC sitting up, staring at the moon. His aura tells me to leave him alone; I do not argue. The song continues.

The song begins to fade. I join him outside, staring at the moon as the melodic, pained voice continues to recite his goodbye to his lover repeats in my short-term. The thick air of clarity coats the grime I've felt since the debacle in Las Vegas. My attention to TC is acute; his head bobs, sways, floats: he's got something to say.

"I have woken up many days feeling as if I'm dead, going through moments as if they mattered. I have so much within, so much to say, but no one has the time to understand or listen. I have wasted my time, writing these thoughts, these poems. For what? You grow up thinking you're going to make a difference. Make some girl happy, make the world better. It just doesn't work out that way. The envelopes I give you... it just closes out the chapters of my life."

His words ring loud, out here in the desert, louder than if he had an amplified microphone; a critter skittles away to some brush, taking any thoughts with it; I continue sitting. I sit because it's obvious I feel the wild gloominess sprouting its roots which holds me, pushes me to continue on this trip, this path, whatever, in order to complete a cycle, a cycle I've felt that wasn't my choice. I have to voice this.

"All these words, poems, songs you have and I read, must be collected and somehow sent to the right people, especially to Allie."

He succumbs to his hands, taking a deep breath.

"Kid, nothing I have ever written, or will ever write, will matter. It's not words on a piece of paper or in a book that matters. It's the passion of who writes the words and how they express the words in the time that they were alive. Planning is not an option."

I lean forward on my knees and take a deep breath. The air is so pure it causes me to cough.

"You understand that me being here is fucking up my life back home. Shit, if we get back home. Who knows what's waiting for us when we get back home, if I get back home. Why don't you just tell me what the game-plan is? Maybe I can help."

I stop talking, stop racking, stop... THINKING! My brain, for whatever grandiose idea there is materializing, is in constant cushion of self-loathing and interest. I need to know because I have to move on. And nature gives me a bump. The moon becomes shrouded in a small puff, canvassing the area in darkness, to re-appear in its luminescence a minute later.

"You never had to stay. You always had the opportunity to leave. You still can. I can drop you off at the next gas station, bus station, whatever. It's no big deal."

I pause for an absolutely quick re-cap of everything.

"No– I want to continue on."

"Good, have you ever been to L.A?"

"Once."

"Wow, just a kid. See any peep shows?"

"No."

He gets up and dusts himself off.

"Well, come on; join me in the land of plastic and status."

I stand, dust myself off and follow him back to the Lincoln.

CHAPTER **20**

WHAT IS REALITY?
CAN YOU MAKE THAT JUDGMENT?

Los Angeles: a mecca of diverse areas, neighborhoods, clichés... like a super-human form of high school without textbooks and with transvestites. I was here when I was 10 years old walking the infinite streets. My fondest, undoubtedly, only remaining memory, was walking past a newsstand that had the first issue of Madonna in Playboy. I trailed behind my parents and the family I was visiting to pick up the magazine and quickly found the section. This was an age where this was not kept in cellophane bags, a time where pornography was not used in court as scapegoats for murder or rape. Such a perverted landscape nowadays; the landscape is quintessential: palm trees, blue skies and maybe one cloud but only if it's union or has an agent. I frequent the entertainment world from friends whom have dived off the board after drinking the kool-aid, with the sneakers on and a roll of quarters in their pockets. The alleged star maps that will take you on a tour of the Star's houses: a unique kitsch where people from outside will pay for tours around a city to drive by houses of people they will never meet. I've been doing that for years back in Ohio. I wonder if I could get away with that here, seeing I have no job and soon, no place to live.

The car ride is slow: traffic is the real citizen of the city. Even with eight lanes of highway and the thru-ways between cars for motorcycles, it never flows. The sun shines bright, holding hands with the ominous smog. TC has dozed off but I continue scanning, glancing, gazing at all the various things to see: billboards, shops, boulevards, electronic billboards, endless cars and stoplights. This city can be suffocating even with the abundant territory it covers. New York City, which I have been many times, at least has concentrated themes; LA is just an amoeba of jelly, this and that with a little of who or what spread over an over-baked toast of land.

The divider comes down.

"TC, we heading to Santa Monica?"

TC wakes up.

"No, Venice Beach."

The divider goes up. TC rubs the sleep from his old, bloodshot eyes; I look away to the splendor of all these businesses, all these tickets for the winning American Dream, some lavish, some poor, some absolutely vivacious, and the women. I don't think I saw one unattractive one on the way. The energy, the tingle is tangible.

"Calm down, it's not a school field trip. Don't cream your pants."

I raise a simple hand; I stop questioning. I've mysteriously grown to like this guy. Respect is there.

The car stops, TC gets out; I follow him. We are dropped off at the Venice Boardwalk. The noise, the people and the activity couldn't match Cleveland except at the end of a Browns game. We walk down a side street to the beach. What a sight. This beach was so large and so deep you thought it was the Sahara. The sheer giddiness of being a kid was emitting from my pores like my alcohol in this sun. I had to calm down. But I just couldn't stop thinking that some of my friends were at jobs back in Cleveland and I was here, standing on Venice Beach, sitting at a concrete table with worn squares from a painted chess board.

"So now what?"

TC slips a small laugh and a smirk.

"How about a pitcher of beer and breakfast?"

"Sounds great."

The Venice Boardwalk: it's like walking through a dream. Is this reality? This place is a circus. I see a 40 year old woman on roller blades blowing into a sea shell, similar to a warrior announcing a battle cry. Her pride on arrival is staggering, efficient, and ignorant. She is stark naked except for electrical tape covering her nipples and, I think, a band-aid and shoe-string for a thong. Mothers cover their young children's eyes, while the fathers play it off as despicable but double-take no less. I notice an African-American midget on a skateboard. His entire body is on the skateboard: no legs, arms short and dorsal, he paddles past. He looks up at me and gives me the thumbs up; does he even have a thumb? The Venice Beach Orchestra, as their sign states, begins to play. Is this an Orchestra? A bunch of bums, in majority's eyes, hitting their hands on bongo drums; however, the beat is contagious and alluring. The leader of the group must be a local. Over-hearing someone, his name is Abraham: he paints pictures with political statements that incite anger. I appreciate his Freedom of speech since it questions the intricate to the simplest. At least he has found an outlet to express himself. His hands, his pants and his shirt are covered with paint. I don't think he's changed clothes in weeks. 'People are Strange' by the Doors was no lie. TC puts his arm around my shoulder.

"Now you know why people call this fucking place La-La Land."

I nod in agreement and follow him to the patio section of the Venice Bistro. We sit in metal lawn furniture that is surprisingly comfortable; traveling so many miles requires a good stretch, the sun on the skin, and a cold pitcher in the waiting sounds perfect. Life is simple right now. It is nice... and... I want to add more... like what friends are doing compared to what I'm doing... but then I sound aloof; I stop.

TC looks over at the orchestra as I look at the menu. A waitress with dark hair and a genuine smile comes over: beauty can be found everywhere.

"Can I take your order?"

TC takes the lead.

"Yes, I'll have two scrambled eggs, sausage, white toast, a pitcher of Budweiser, two glasses of water and a plastic cup."

"And you sir?"

"I'll have the same, minus the pitcher part. One is fine right now, thanks."

Her genuine smile is the best I can quickly denote her; I bet she appreciates what she has. Then I think of my Vegas gambling. A million thoughts enter my head as we wait but I subside with Abraham's artistic views. Political outrage runs thick & thin in my blood. I find no impetus to sacrifice the bourgeoisie on his or their escapades of decadence and redundancy and verbose bodily rhythms but they should keep their expressions, opinions fixed, immutable, much like the social caste in life. In my learning, I always found the irony in the republic starting in the seeds of the democracy. I twitch my head to stop thinking such frivolous shit.

The waitress comes with a tray: a pitcher of Budweiser, two frozen glasses, two glasses of water and a plastic cup. She sets it all on the table and leaves... with a smile just for me. TC pushes the pitcher to me.

"You know what, the performance of action in a painting, a story, song or poem, should be perceived by the individual who reads or sees it."

This moment is busted by his statement: such serendipity and needless attachments ruined by the thoughtful, provoking statements, that I, as a fellow believer in art, cannot let go without a statement. My ferocious agreement cannot wait to be expressed.

"I agree."

TC stands up and pours a fresh glass of beer into his plastic cup. I'm too tired to convince him to sit down, I just want to relax. I'm too tired to win this argument in public. His words vaporize as the Venice Beach Orchestra tunes up as I turn... for the worse. I have to answer the question of, 'I must be losing my mind', because, suddenly, I'm thinking.

"I'm thinking out loud. Venice, California"

It's okay... until the first person notices.

A soldier in fatigues suddenly storms the beach towards me in full ops like Normandy. My escapism has left me with no relocation of how Beverly Hills 90210 would react, so my mind goes to Venice Beach Survival... of... um, 90210- I think. The six-foot five soldier, thinking he's Patton, stares at me. His fiery fragility creates and demolishes all in his stare, the adrenaline rush of warfare cannot be calmed by cheap street drugs or free beer from liberated Americans. He is a marvelously conflicted soul: from his sanguine anecdotes to his dizzying displays of self-mutilation across his temple with his 'special-issue' knife. The dehumanizing disability in fatigues deliberately walks away from my ignorance of reaction: I simply had no protection or money to give. His reality is layered by my mind culling the song by Samuel Barber's "Adagio for Strings" as he heads over the dunes of Venice Beach to sleep under the Santa Monica pier; O. Stone would understand, because-- I'm losing my mind. Really. A homely couple of tourists interrupt my nascent to transcendence. I turn around with a scowl to the random talkers.

"Who the fuck was that guy, doesn't he know it's America?"

"They should send that fuck back to the Middle East."

Sarge could have portrayed a gruesome act of violence and not cared because he wasn't considered a celebrity, but what the fuck is a celebrity? Is it a presumed affront to our sensibility? It just permits our culture for adults to play like children. The talking Opinions leave...

TC reaches into his pocket, unfolds a sheet of paper, briefly scans the table, walks around the rope rail. Approaching Abraham with an extended hand proves my point: he was here before... yes? They embrace briefly; then hands the paper as if new directives for Abraham. He goes over the sheet; TC sits next to him on the concrete island, strongly presenting the image that TC's sat on that concrete island with pride. Whatever it is, I'm left here, in the bistro, to wonder, so I pour a glass of beer and aimlessly zone off... Stop! Not here and not again! Just sit, and the waitress will show up with her genuine smile. A vibe of telepathy articulates while she places the food down. She nods and leaves; I nod too, but end the telepathy awkwardly. Again, I shake out of it. TC comes over to the railing and pours himself another beer. He grabs his plate, speaking, as he devours his breakfast.

"Why are you so uptight? Relax, let down your shoulders. LA is LA for a reason. Everyone outside of LA thinks it's great. And everyone inside LA knows it's not."

He walks away with the beer in his hand and points back at me.

"Until you do this."

TC joins the Venice Beach Orchestra, grabs a microphone.

"I am Ted Christopher and this is the Venice Beach Orchestra."

A sense of proud follows; I just sit back with my beer... and wait.

"This song is called 'Madness'. I wrote this many, many, many, years ago."

Explosion of all drums beating together leads into a two-minute rhythm duet. TC closes his eyes and bounces his right foot with the tempo.

"I am the Cleveland DJ, Wolf Man Jack, on 98.5 FM re-incarnated. It's his stage."

MAD DRIVE ON THE HIGHWAY!
'Killers' in the background,
GOODWILL FOR THE FUTURE,
Splash in the ocean

{The Bongo drums become louder}

DIG DEEP… IN THE SOUL-WHOLE
RUN FREE… IN THE SUN-HUN
FLY BY… IN THE SKY-HIGH
DIVE IN… THE SEA-HE

{The Bongo drums refrain}

Beaver trap hunt'nnn
Oh-yeah hunt'nnn
Beaver trap hunt'nnn
Oh-yeah hunt'nnn

{The bongo drums pick up the pace}

LAY
Lay… in the field
SEARCH
Search… for the stars
DRIFT
Drift… in the wind
PLAY
Play… by the river

{The bongo drums refrain}

Beaver trap hunt'nnn
Oh-yeah hunt'nnn
Beaver trap hunt'nnn
Oh-yeah hunt'nnn

{The bongo drums pick up the pace}

JUMP
Jump… in the river
SWIM
Swim… through the clouds
LIVE
Live… in the moment
LIVE
Live… in the dream

{Mad Congo – a collection of bongo drums, triangles, and morocco's}
Beaver trap hunt'nnn
OH-YEAH HUNT'NNN

BEAVER TRAP HUNT'NNN
Oh-yeah hunt'nnn

BEAVER TRAP HUNT'NNN
OH-YEAH HUNT'NNN

TC drops the microphone and laughs with the orchestra. He shakes hands with all the members and throws a hundred dollar bill in the open guitar case. The tourist walk by; the locals clap. I watch in disbelief as he returns to the table. He just sits back, with his hands behind his head, gleaming smile in tow.

"You only live once, my friend. What I just did will

never be understood as entertainment. It doesn't seem to matter. The only entertainment coming out of Hollywood these days is porn and cartoons. At least you know they're acting. I'll be back."

TC enters the Bistro. As I sit back and ponder the relevance behind the truth, the beer is going down smooth, California smooth. I fill my glass again and go back into this nonsense of thought: the where-am-I, what-am-I-doing, will-this-ever-make-sense, crap. Fuck that shit; I want to get deep down into it, down to the root. The root of the problem is where it began, where it all exists, landing on his yard is still a lingering virus on my brain. But business, simple economics, and life continue to function as a balancing power, a seating chart. It's a valet parking lot, with a Ferrari pulling into a sea of cars as a shark patrolling for blood. You don't have to live here to know that the presumption of guilt is stoked by the countless meanderings of shrewd deception. Predator and prey: who are you?

TC returns to the table and hands me a sheet of notebook paper.

"See that bench beyond the boardwalk?"

"Yeah"

"Sit there and enjoy the read."

"Why there?"

"The title will answer that."

I attempted to pause but I listened, and, before I knew it, I was already sitting there. The sun is scorching hot, noon is coming. Girls and boys ride skateboards, scooters, razors, while men and women are on bikes or roller blades. They all fly by on this man-made street that out-lines the beach. I look towards the ocean: surfers; I look at the expansive beach: volleyball nets and players. Everyone seems to be having fun, exercising, active. I look down at the sheet and read:

I REMEMBER

I Remember
Feeling... Light
Against my skin

Feeling... Alive

I Remember
Feeling... Wind
Beneath my feet

Feeling... Free

I Remember
Hearing... Music
In my dream

Hearing... The Song

I Remember
Hearing... Laughter
In a crowd

Hearing... Applause

I Remember
Seeing... Stars
In my universe

Seeing... Magic

I Remember
Seeing... A Girl
In my heart

Seeing... Love

I Remember...

I Remember
Feeling... So Free- Alive

I Remember
Hearing... The Laughter and Song

I Remember
Seeing... The Beauty- The Girl

LOVE

I Remember...

I Remember
Being... A Kid

A horn blares; Monyak pulls up. Amazing: to have such transportation makes me think of a magic carpet. The five hundred feet I run is nothing; I feel like its home once I land on the leather seats. TC hits down the divider.

"Monyak, to Pacific and Dudley, just look for the rainbow doors. Pull over and put on your hazards."

The Lincoln takes off and stops about a minute later; what's the point? TC gets out and I follow, as always. He knocks on a purple door, Apartment F. I stand back and wait, anticipating the climax I've grown accustomed to in TV shows: he probably has a vendetta against somebody and wants to end it at this moment, hour, this day. I always wanted a gun.

A girl answers in a black t-shirt and sweat pants. Her five-foot three height with dark hair and fair skin complements her hair as a mess: she has style without style.

"I'm sorry to bother you. I am... Ted Christopher and I used to live her a long time ago."

"Nice to meet you, I'm Samantha."

"I know how it is to live here in L.A. How much is one months' rent?"

"It's about ten-fifty a month."

His smirk has me on edge.

"How about I give you 1200 dollars, for say... an hour in this apartment?"

"Are you kidding me?"

"No."

She blanks out, speechless, just as I am; TC walks back to the Lincoln. Monyak rolls down the window and hands him an envelope. TC returns with 12 hundred dollar bills in his hand. He hands the money to Samantha. It's a beautiful thing to see, her legs shake and her lips quiver.

"You have no idea how much this helps me out. I want to be an artist and my boyfriend is a struggling musi-"

"Trust me. I know; it's L.A."

She grabs her purse and keys.

"There is pop, juice and beer in the little fridge. Take your time, just lock the door behind you and slam it shut."

She walks away. TC walks back to the Lincoln and hands Monyak a hundred dollar bill.

"Davy Jones Locker, it's the second stop light, to the left. Be there in about five hours. In the meantime, pick up some hot fucking blonde; you have a Lincoln."

Monyak pulls away and we enter 101 Dudley, Apt F. TC walks around in amazement, actually excited. He walks into the bathroom. I do not share his enthusiasm. This is a piece of shit. One room, with a bathroom, carpet as thin as deli-sliced ham, a ceiling fan that went at a speed that bets could be taken which direction it would spin off and decapitate any occupant. A trundle bed left behind by the current tenant because she is probably on tour every other week with her current boyfriend. The backseat of the Lincoln is a much better place is my assessment; at least you can roll down the window. TC breaks my melancholy mood.

"The same fucking bed, unbelievable."

He opens the fridge and throws me a Bud Light. He cracks open his beer and sits on the end of the bed.

"A friend from back home made the trip with me. We spent six months of our lives living here. This bed right here was amazing. It pulled out, so he had one half and I had the other. We lived like shit and let our family and friends believe that we were living like kings. He had a film degree from Cleveland State. I had nothing but a car and a dream. Put it this way, he believed, truly believed in my masterpiece."

TC polishes off his beer and cracks open another one.

"We spent about five thousand dollars creating T-shirts. We had five hundred black and white shirts promoting the masterpiece. You could wear these shirts inside out. On the inside, was a solid cross; on the other side was a cross with part of the title written inside. On the back was the rest of the title, with this necklace and cross transposed."

TC shows me the cross around his neck. He starts opening up cupboards and closets.

"I would hang pictures of dark haired girls that I thought could be Hope. I would write stupid little statements, like: 'Ted, where are you.' I wasn't insane; it just helped to make the dream a reality."

I finish my beer and go in the fridge for another one.

"No, we need to get going."

"You just paid twelve-hundred dollars for this place."

"No big deal, it's just money."

I close the fridge and follow him outside. I slam the door shut, he just laughs. We take a quick right and walk a side street. We cross a parking lot and stop at a street sign, Main Street and Rose. The light changes, we head down Main Street. TC is like a tour guide. He points out the bar across the street.

"The Firehouse- good burgers... and beers are relatively cheap."

We continue to walk, passing by a hair salon and a Pilates building. Women come out the door displaying their new posture or mat.

"It's California. Everybody is worried about their looks."

Just then, a woman, about twenty-three, comes out of Baja Fresh. Her skin, her persona is something I have never seen before. She wears a short skirt and black converse shoes that tie all the way up to her knees. The kind of style you do not find back in the East. I don't know what to do, so I light up a smoke. We continue on and pass the Chaya, on Main Street and Navy. The glass windows reveal that TC and I in a pair of jeans and the T-shirt would not be welcomed. A limo pulls up and it's not Monyak. Four women exit with an aura of LA. The high heels and Rodeo Drive aurally drift money. It's not Wal-Mart; it's Christian Louboutin. TC smiles and motions.

"Hello."

They look: at him, as if he was a bum living on the beach. I can tell this kind of shit bothers him. We walk on and I see something amazing, beautiful. It's like a scene from a movie or that playboy pictorial I saw when I was ten. This women in a sun dress and the sexiest shoes I ever seen walks towards us. She has no makeup on and a white flower in her hair. She has golden brown hair, succulent lips and aqua colored eyes, even though she wears sunglasses. She moves, flows with radiance and confidence. TC is blown away. One thing I know about him: he appreciates beauty and art.

"I love your shoes. I love your dress. I love your style."

She doesn't even acknowledge his existence.

"You know what."

She turns around with an attitude. This tension could crack ice.

"That dress and your legs will definitely get you laid. But no man will ever love you for who you are. Please, look in the mirror and change who you are."

She turns around in her grass-hopper sunglasses, ignorant to the words that came out of his mouth. With a shrug, he grabs my shoulder.

"You can always tell when you're in LA... I have a car, let's go get it."

He walks away in another direction all proud. And I laugh to myself because of the magnitude of tangents this man works from. You have to have a car in LA. And then, as a child, I wonder to myself, seeing this guy is full of surprises, does he have a Bentley or an old Rolls in a parking garage?

I casually follow behind his pace because I've gotten to the point of why he has morphed into a malignant tumor. I simply will just follow until he dies. I admit to my sheepishness. But I can't care anymore. I see he turns a corner into a skyscraper but it's actually a concrete garage. After a couple floors of steps and an elevator built by a boy scout, he shows his car.

"My charcoal Ford Focus. What a sweet ride."

After a minute of TC's telepathy with his 'sweet ride', he gets in, grabs a black t-shirt from the glove compartment and puts it on. His sarcasm level is off the charts so I just nod. He unlocks my door; I get in. I attempt to change the radio station but he stops me.

"Sorry, only the CD works. Listen to this."

It starts off slow but it builds to 'On The Turning Away' by Pink Floyd. I love this song. I actually don't think as he shifts into drive and ventures into the streets of Santa Monica. I have a minute to myself without his talking and my shadow thoughts. The vocals transcend me to an ethereal place. I love it. Especially in this jungle. But my musical feed is short-lived. A cop pulls us over within two minutes. I immediately feel cheated, screwed, at where this finish line is.

The sequence goes like this:

He shows license: it's Ohio.

Insurance: glove compartment.

"Come with me."

TC gets out.

They both stop behind the car; he administers a DUI test.

I slap myself. This many miles for a lesson learned-but the cop points to his chest. The words

T

STRUGGLE

H

E

are written inside a cross.

They talk for hours it feels.

I sit and try to watch with a better angle in the side view mirror.

The cop goes back to his car and comes back with TC's license.

They shake hands.

They split ways.

TC gets in. I'm beside myself.

TC slowly gets accustomed to the steering wheel and seat. The cop pulls out into the street and passes. TC lets out his own breath.

"Never underestimate the power of faith."

He points at the cross on his T-shirt.

"Why? What happened?"

"He said he could not arrest a man of faith. His mother would disown him."

I relax back into the seat. I want to ask more questions. I should but I don't because... I'm selfish. We enter a Ford dealership. TC tells me to wait across the street. I don't argue since there's a coffee-shop and the dealer showcase is all windows. So I quickly sit with my coffee in hand and watch. But I don't. I drift into my head because of the ebullience of Santa Monica: its buildings draped in sparkle and razz-ma-tazz, how it glitters on everyone's affliction of Monday afternoon. But we all strut the sidewalk like a carnival, providing the artificiality of actors in drama class. Our reasons have less to do with our antics than with our consequences from strangers: from the continuous walk-bys, the rotation of their heads, to the fluttering, flexing of their hand, finger gestures, really? I conjure up the sharply poignant coincidence of approaching an observed tourist and his child-like authenticity. I want to remind this to a tourist who takes pictures of every movable, slippery part. I want to tell him or her that not everything can be ingested at once. He or she can come back for more, but I know, either or, will scoff or complain.

TC taps on my shoulder and displays a check, pocketing it before I can see the amount- a rush of blood and caffeine makes me jump up. I wish we could cash his check and not have to walk. That person of complete mediocrity decides to speak to us: a tourist. It's got to be.

"I know you LA types, your righteousness is smarter than my enjoyment of pictures, violent or not. You can't fool anyone in here."

I stand dumb-founded with my coffee in hand and witness TC, trying to cash the check next door, which eventually turns into three different banks and thirty minutes. TC walks out empty-handed.

"Credit and a good check in this place don't matter. This place is unbelievable. Fucking garbage."

I just follow him... all the way to Main Street in Venice. Couldn't we have just got a cab?

Another drink drank, another block walked, and another thought confuses: life is just pieces that we are lucky to grab and throw in the basket of consciousness. To read and to feel TC's romantic epiphanies is to push self-conscious into a vague core of sexuality, purism, and social engineering. His blizzard of valentines is blinding but simple from the same ingredient: white, cold truth. I know of the cheap confections that decorate others' attempts, being my previous attempts, but come up with only saccharine and flavorless. So I stopped because of the tiresome attempt to be original. Every sweet slice of life became a diagram of technical writing seen in the instructions of putting a desk together. Maybe my yielding to my anxiety would not have disrupted or disoriented the recipient, my love at the time. To calibrate a flawless soliloquy is foolish, just as the criticism I received. However the amorous intensity was there, bred from the throes of my lust and longing, maybe if I was more relaxed and engaging, I wouldn't have yearned for such an anti-climatic feeling. Andy Warhol said, 'Think rich, look poor'. How untypical it would be, on a billboard here in LA. We have congressional ethics and corruption, clash over drugs, tornadoes in committee selections for health-care, and then, I see a white-tailed deer in a beautiful, budding actress walk by, I think of the armed predator, bow and arrow in tow, ready to strike and take down this dreaming doe, minus the John Williams soundtrack.

LA can be a fairy tale of indoctrination, littered with Freud's wet dreams of sexual virginity, dark fears, and grand desires. What a subversion of the cultural norms. Thank God I grew up on the North Coast. What did TC think? Did he leave behind his family and friends and discover a suffocating social system of unfair, malevolent cheats, and apathetic broken souls? Have his frivolous words and thoughts leaded him astray? Should I do the same, sell my soul so I can, at the least, get past the velvet rope of other meaningless specters? Maybe I should live on in a mind of I-don't-know. Do everything with an I-don't-know fueling the actions so no agenda is motivating me. Where are the people you read about that bring fruitions of real art, real pioneers of expanding upon the syntheses of individuality's of the same external stimuli, the same environments but with clever, thoughtful re-arrangements? That's right: they're hidden in their ivory towers awaiting their next call from their publicist to do a radio/talk-show/tabloid appearance. On the way, we pass a chalk-board of a dive coffee-house. In chalk, 'Open Mic- Poetry Night'. That would have been good for all his poems or songs. The smartest things are usually the simplest... and easiest.

CHAPTER **21**

TO THE DREAMERS WHO DREAM

We cross a street and enter a bar called 'O'Brien's Irish Pub'. Finally. What a stupid walk when we could've... bah, my brain aches. TC went straight to the bar and gets two Budweiser's. I stand and watch a series of motor cross accidents on the TV screen. That's entertainment? I follow him outside to the patio. We sit and drink quietly as the everyday afternoon of California passes by.

"See the sky?"

"Yeah, it's clear, and?"

"Well, that's how it is every day. You wake up and walk outside and see that it's the same old day. People envy this, but if you live here for a while, you envy the seasons."

"Yeah, but this I can get used to."

"No, you don't want this shit."

"Why wouldn't I?"

He shakes his head as if I haven't learned a thing.

"Reality TV shows are pretty big right now, right?"

I chug the brew and nod.

"I would love to take ten people that grew up and lived in LA, and make the switch with ten people from Cleveland. The middle of winter, you know what I mean?"

I drink and ponder the idea. It's not bad; it would definitely sell. I did notice that: if you can sell, you can sell anything in this city. Hell, why do the studios feel they have to be here anyway?

"You know what, fuck the reality show. Take a half-million people from Cleveland, Buffalo, and Detroit and replace it with a half-million people from here."

He takes a big swig. His pauses are so grandiose.

"I will tell you this; the city bars wouldn't be dead at 10 pm."

"You saying this area is dead by 10 pm?"

He simply nods in grand motion. Now I shake my head. He stops me short.

"Do me a favor, talk to the bartender and find out why the owner has certain movie posters hanging on the wall. Why 'Aviator', why 'Ali'?

He hands me twenty bucks, so I figure why not. I'm such a whore when free money's involved. So I talk to the bartender in the best matter-of-fact style to find out he's the owner. I come back with two Budweiser's and the answer.

"He's not the bartender, he's the owner. His good friend and business partner of the bar produced those movies."

"Figures, everyone knows everyone. Why don't I know anyone?"

He finishes the next bottle in complete speed, places another twenty underneath his bottle and walks away. I truly want to stay and enjoy, but I have no idea where I am, so I chug at a faster speed and follow him down the street, entering a bar called Rick's. He orders two Budweiser's and sits at a table across from the bar. I join him and we drink. I look around and gaze at all the Yankee memorabilia and wonder where I am. TC looks confused; he stares at his beer bottle. I know I shouldn't but I do.

"You all right?"

"Yeah, see the girl at the end of the bar?"

"Yeah, she's good looking."

"Find out her story."

"Why?"

"Everyone has a story."

I must admit, this shit is getting weird, but on some level I feel empowered, I can do anything since I didn't live here. I walk over to the end of the bar and sit next to her.

"Sorry to bother you, I'm from Cleveland and I have no idea what I'm doing here. But that Old Man back there thinks you have a story. You can slap me in the face or tell me to leave and I'll understand."

The bartender laughs.

"She goes by the name of Renee. Right now she is a back-up singer to one of the greatest acts in the world."

"And who are you?"

"Just a bartender."

She laughs.

"Come on, JP, you're more than just a bartender."

TC throws two hundred dollars on the bar.

"You guys split this; I wish I could give you more. I can see it. You are both honest and good."

He walks out of the bar. Again, I want to stay but I have to go.

"Nice meeting you two, good luck, good luck."

I run across the street to follow him into the World Café. We sit inside the lounge: an airy, exploratory designing of the world in a blender but it flows based on ottomans and chaises. A waitress with light black skin and personality comes and takes our order. TC looks up at her name tag.

"Hello, Maria, we will have two double shots of Patron and two chasers of grapefruit juice."

She leaves.

"So how do you like California?"

"I think LA is a separate territory from California. Plus... the girls are different."

"They are, so are the girls back home. I have to go to the bathroom. Find out what Maria is all about."

"What?"

"Ask the questions. How else can you find out information?"

He leaves; I get defensive; Maria enters. She places down the drinks and smiles.

"Um, well, I can tell you're humble, but what is your true passion in life?"

"I'm not sure what you mean?"

"What do you want to do? No reason not to be honest."

"Okay- I'm a waitress here, in LA, and, yes, I want to be an actress. I take drama classes on the weekends and I was the lead in a theater play last year."

"How did that go?"

"It was amazing. Halle Berry showed up at the premiere. She gave me a hug and said that I was brilliant. Even made her tear up a bit. But, I still have to work here and I still have to worry about paying my bills, but that moment made all of my dreams worthwhile."

"How often do people ask you about your dreams?"

She looks up at the ceiling for maybe a pasted answer.

"You know what... not often."

She winks and leaves as a young girl hauls in music equipment: speakers, amplifiers, a microphone and a guitar case. She sets up in the corner of the café. TC comes back with two mixed drinks. I relay the warm response from Maria and her whole situation. He just smiles as if he knows. The drinks, for some reason, are going down well. I actually feel accomplished today in this jungle. TC just looks at the young girl and shakes his head in obvious disappointment: a pin to my bubble.

"Now what?"

"That girl is talented. She is on her own. She is going after her dream. She hauls her equipment around and plays for the reason to play, not obligations. She has passion, heart, real reason- it's her dream, it's her purpose."

She starts rehearsing, tuning her guitar and singing. I look over at TC's face exuding the kind of expression a father does on college graduation for his daughter. I turn my head to see... we're the only two people in the lounge... and she is the personal entertainment. He hands me the mixed drink.

"Find out her name and where she is from."

I still sigh every time he says shit like that, but I figure he's paid for this entire trip and I have another cold beverage of top shelf liquor in my hand, so I walk over and utilize my new founded charm.

"My friend and I were wondering how long you have been in California?"

She is quite cordial and has a beautiful smile. I know why TC is excited. She is about five-foot two carrying long, dark hair that probably takes an hour to brush. I feel she is a reminder of his high school sweetheart. I just do. She stops plugging in her speaker.

"I've been here for about a year."

"It sounds like you have an accent. Where you from?"

"I moved here from England... it's been tough."

"Do you have many friends around here?"

"I made a few, but they will never replace the friends I have back home."

"You haul around the equipment alone?"

"Some days are tougher than others, but it's worth it. Playing guitar and singing is my passion. I enjoy coming here and playing or playing at the Promenade in Santa Monica. Yes, I am human I would love to sign a big contract and play in the greatest concert halls, but right now, I'm happy, and if that never happens, I'll still be happy, because I love what I do."

"You have an amazing attitude. Glad to have met you."

I extend my hand oafishly, but she introduces herself.

"I'm Carrie Ann."

"Well, hello, Carrie Ann. Honored."

"And you are?"

"Oh, just a new fan."

I walk away and join TC back at the table. He can see my enthusiasm. I tell him her story and he just smiles, hanging upon every word I say. He throws a hundred dollar bill on the table and we finish our drinks. He then walks over to Carrie and pulls out a money clip. He shakes hands with her and hands her a wad of money. I watch and can't believe how much money he is giving away. I appreciate him seeing her passion; her struggle, I understand, but, I want to go over and say 'What the fuck? What about me?' — but I'm enjoying this discovery of engagement with strangers too much. I squelch the ego in me; TC leaves without a word from me. I'm hoping he says something.

We walk a side street and reach Pacific. We cross the street and I see the Lincoln parked at Davy Jones Locker. Monyak is one hell of a chauffeur. We jump in the back. TC hits down the divider.

"Monyak to CAA and Endeavor."

The drive from Venice to CAA is a letdown and, for the first time, I do not want to exit the car. Monyak hands three envelopes to TC, all titled 'The Hollywood Creed'. He leads; I follow him into this intimidating building of sheer indulgence of architecture and overinvestment. The suits that walk in and out, the women in their seven inch heels: it's a perception to keep their constituents, the ticket-buyers, possible dreamers, out. He walks straight up to the front desk.

"Excuse me, where is the basement."

The receptionist is dumbfounded.

"Why... why do you want to go to the basement?"

TC leans over the desk, looking directly at her.

"Because I know you will never let me see an agent."

She laughs, seeing the envelopes in his hand, as if she knows her job and knows he is right.

"Well, we only accept solicited material. We do not accept unsolicited material."

He just laughs.

"Well, I guess it still doesn't matter if the material is good or bad."

She points him the direction. He walks to the elevator and I have to follow as he hits the button with a big letter B. The simple knife-pointed stare he gave her was worth it. And as we arrive in the basement: there are no balloons, no skateboarders doing tricks, no juggling clowns, or even doves... but just a basement, a basement garage filled with BMWs, Porches, Lamborghinis, Ferraris, Bentleys. He walks into the mail room and hands an employee an envelope. I just watch, wondering why he is wasting his time. We take the stairs and exit the building. The silence is stoic and needed. I can feel some sort of telepathy oozing from him: the penultimate hatred of this existence, to walk into to this building, is the antithesis of his very existence.

I simply follow him to the Lincoln and drive over to Endeavor for the duplication of the same routine; but this time, I stay in the car. TC comes back out and slams into the backseat. Monyak rolls down the window, awaiting.

"Monyak, just take me to a place where I can see the sign!"

We drive. I go into my head but stop short because of the sour dour on TC's face. It's like he just went into battle with a Minotaur. Amazing how such a free spirit can be sucked dry by the vacuum of futility. It sucks. All of a sudden, Monyak slams on the brakes. TC hands me the last letter and exits the car. He sits on a city bench and stares at the Hollywood Sign on the hill. I open the letter titled 'The

Hollywood Creed,' and read:

The Hollywood Creed

It's not about
Money
It's about
Being happy

It's not about
Fame
It's about
Being artistic

It's not about
Winning or losing
It's about
Being honorable

It's not about
An academy award – the spotlight
It's about
Being human

It's not about
America and third world countries
It's about
Being real and doing what's right

It's not about
War, democracy and hate
It's about
Peace, love and forgiveness

One life
That's all we have
And that's all that matters.

I finish. And. I discover time moving faster than ever

before. Led Zeppelin had a song, 'Going to California', and I think I just got punched in the nose and the blood is flowing. I look and see no blood, but living has taken its toll: drinking all the time, the money evaporating on smokes, beer, drinks, useless invitations to bars; the lessons are morphing leaner, meaner, causing the loneliness, the void of community within a metropolis, to a point where volume of comedy is... gone. The weather causes a loss of time, is it 4pm, no, that was two hours ago. Is he in my head?

I shake out of my internal surfing and am told of a meal at Decks. The picturesque ride on Highway 1 is replaced with a large, picturesque window of Monyak, TC and I sitting, all looking out at the surf. The Pacific Ocean is literally below my sight. I watch a school of dolphins swim by; I immediately feel like I'm at Sea World in Aurora, Ohio: a place I remember going with my parents when I was a child. TC orders two bottles of Dom Perignon and three steaks: the best steaks in the house; three salads with thousand island dressing; lobster tail on the side, and while we're waiting, two rum and cokes plus a Budweiser... bottled.

The dinner is served; the conversation is flowing with the champagne down the gullets. TC chews and swallows his last bite. He holds his glass of champagne in the air.

"A dream: to leave your family, to leave your friends, to leave everything you know behind. You have to be willing to walk alone, to become unknown, to not have a home. Is it worth it? Is it good to have a dream?"

"To have a dream is normal, but to lose all that you have is a problem. You need a back-up plan, a plan B."

"True, but what if you go against your morals, in essence sell your soul?"

"Everything is a sale, don't take it literally. Money opens doors for repair."

"A minor league baseball player may use steroids to make it to the major leagues or a major league player may use roids to become the best. Is being the best worth the cost?

"Ball players have never paid my bills and never will. So I really don't care."

"You're missing the point; the soul, the human heart, the overall experience of being alive. The greatest writers throughout history understood their point, their purpose. Dante's – Inferno. Milton's – Paradise Lost. Thoreau's – Walden Pond. Whitman's – Leaves of Grass. Shakespeare's – Hamlet. Salinger's – Catcher in The Rye. Hemingway's – Old Man and the Sea. Look at me."

I look at him.

"I wrote my masterpiece for a reason. A writer believes his redemption in life can be performed on stage in a one night only event. Someday those words will make sense to you."

"Why these pieces? They are considered timeless, untouchable."

TC laughs.

"What does 'Field of Dreams', 'The Last of the Mohicans', 'Titanic', and 'Braveheart', have in common?"

I eat my last bite and savor the best meal I've had in years.

"No clue."

Monyak puts down his glass.

"James Horner."

I wash the steak down with the tingling sensation of champagne.

"Who is that?"

Monyak laughs.

"The best composer since Beethoven, and he never used steroids."

Monyak fervently follows with a face of stone. TC holds up his glass of champagne.

"What we take for granted. It's like hot water in a shower. The average American has no idea how the water becomes hot. They just expect it."

He finishes the glass. Monyak and I just stare at him and wonder what he is thinking. TC shakes his head.

"A writer must be able to adapt, throw away old ideas and begin again. A writer must create new visions, new frontiers and new ideas. This trip was not about love, friendship, or family. It was about burying the hatchet that tore apart my soul."

TC pays for the bill. And as we are leaving tells Monyak,

"Mariasol."

On the way to the Lincoln, I hear a car unloading people, but the people didn't pique my attention, it was the over-excessive volume of a song: 'Rise' by Pantera. I love the parallels of life.

CHAPTER **22**

TO END WHERE IT BEGAN

The back of the Lincoln is somber: I'm busy with that song in my head, TC might have larger ideas for the night and Monyak, well, who knows what he thinks: he might be imagining himself working in Maine. TC hands me an envelope titled: MASTERPIECE.

"This is not my masterpiece; it's just a simple poem, song, whatever. Read it out loud."

I laugh to myself of its self-aggrandizement; I open the envelope, unfold the sheet and decide to read the poem out loud.

A MASTERPIECE

To be born
...To grow up

And see

A sanctuary
Of beauty

A masterpiece

Where water
Flows through valley's
As mountains
Tower over seas

Where leaves
Scatter across grass
As snow
Falls upon fields

Where flowers
Bloom into spring
As a sun
Rises in the sky

Close your eyes
Imagine

A sanctuary
Of art

A MASTERPIECE

TC stares at the ocean through the window. He takes the helm by finishing the rest of the poem from memory. I just listen.

She sat on
A wooden chair
In an empty low lit room

She had on
 A black gown, a white veil
And red lipstick

Her bare feet
And tiny toes
Touched the hardwood floor below

She was innocent
Yet strong

Her
Straight dark hair
Draped over her eyes

Her
Smooth light skin
…Radiated.

A MASTERPIECE

She smiled…
Then looked up at me…
And said…
…I love you

TC looks at me and smiles. He continues to recite the words as I look down upon this sheet of paper in my hands.

The touch
Of her hand
Made me quiver

The sight
Of her bare back
Made me turn around

But the sound
…The sound
Of her laugh

Made me…

Made me…

Never want…
  To go to sleep.

He quiets down as we pull up, parking on the Santa Monica Pier. The legality of some these stunts have numbed to even thinking they're wrong. TC gets out and I follow him into a bar called the Mariasol. He orders a Budweiser and I choose a Corona as a step up from the norm. We don't say a word to one another. I must admit, throughout the duration of this trip, I have become comfortable in living this way of nonsense and non-linear understanding, fragmented at the least. At first I thought he would be more of a mentor, but after I got to know him, he became more of a friend. He finishes his beer, pays for the drinks and tells me to meet him outside when I am finished. He walks out the side door and disappears. I savor the last few ounces of the good beer and walk out the side door and disappear. I find him sitting at the top of the bleacher steps at the end of the pier. It's a beautiful sight. An older man sits alone with a guitar and covers a classic song by Bob Dylan called 'Not Dark Yet'. I join TC at the top of the bleachers and sit down. The Pacific Ocean and the vastness of thought it creates in my head is the reason for really living. It doesn't make sense but it makes sense now. We just sit there in complete silence. I listen to the music and watch as the red glow in the sky sets over Malibu. The music ends and this old man covering Dylan walks away. TC looks at the moon; it's faint in the sky, as if a lace transposes its visibility.

"The moon, simply beautiful, amazing; somewhere out there is a little girl named Allie, my sweetheart. I know she sees the same moon tonight. I just know."

He puts his hand on my shoulder.

"Never take anything for granted."

He throws in a chew, I light up a smoke and we walk pass the Ferris wheel and the roller coaster, families laughing, high school dates with the uncomfortable silences.

Monyak opens the back door and we jump inside. I make a Gin and Tonic to cap the vision; TC cracks open a Budweiser.

"Monyak, it's time, you know the destination."

TC closes the divider and we drive towards Venice Beach.

"I hope you don't think this trip was a waste of your time, because everything in this crazy world has a purpose. There was a reason you passed out drunk in my front yard. I thought when this all began that I would help show you the way, and in some aspect, save your life. It's funny or ironic; it's like looking in the rear view mirror and seeing it all over again. Bottom line kid, you have passion and that is all that matters in life. Without knowing it, you have taught me something. If I told you, you would just laugh because you are still too young and dumb to understand. I know that pisses you off because you're a stubborn fool, but it's the truth. Just know that you made a difference in my life."

He laughs and shakes his head.

"Well, the end is near, so I might as well tell you. I was born on April 23rd and I always thought I would die on April 23rd. I don't know, it's a stupid thing like Shakespeare and I have this eternal bond in destiny or something on those lines. Yeah, I know, he wrote Hamlet, Macbeth, Romeo and Juliet. And I wrote some stupid little poems. But, in the end, it really doesn't matter."

He cracks open another Budweiser. I look down, amazed that I finished my drink during his rant; I make another one.

"On April 23rd, next year, is your final mission. After that you will be ready."

I must admit, I am kind of lost. I did not completely realize that I have been on missions.

"Ready for what? What's this final mission?"

He starts laughing.

"It's not like finding the Holy Grail or saving Africa. It's simply just showing up.

9:23 P.M, Huntington Beach, Ohio, on April 23rd."

He hands me an envelope titled, 'ALLIE'.

"You're a smart kid; you will know when to open it."

He rubs his tired eyes with such strength that I want to reach out and stop him.

"Life is strange. Over the years, I lost myself. The heaven I once saw turned into hell. You get to a point in your life where you don't know who you are anymore. You don't know where you are going or where you have been. You talk to your family and you talk to your friends. You act like everything in your life is okay. You act as if you are living the dream. You know that kind of shit. The truth - I'm hurting. And nobody knows it, because I am stubborn."

TC wipes a tear from his eye and looks up at me.

"Just remember this: society will put a hold on you. People in the industry believe they know what's right. Egos translate into a superficial power. Doing what's right, doing what's wrong, doing what is accepted. Money does not mean success. Follow your heart- no matter what the cost... just follow your heart. Be bold. Don't doubt. Words are great, but they don't mean a thing without action. The most important thing: the less you have, the less you have to worry about."

Monyak skids to a stop in the Venice Beach parking lot. TC grabs a bottle of Jack

Daniels and three shot glasses and exits the car. He sets the glasses on the hood of the car and pours three healthy portions. Monyak, TC and I grab the shots as TC speaks.

"To be intelligent is a gift; but to be compassionate and understanding allows you to open that gift."

He then raises his shot like a national trophy.

"Alcohol... is like a cancer. It can kill a dream."

The shots go down easy; we all laugh for no reason and smile, but then TC gets serious, he shakes both of our hands.

"If I never see you guys again, then good luck. That's it and that's that. Monyak, in five minutes, cue the music."

I'm pretty much lost at this point; add confusion and nervousness and that's me. TC walks onto the beach. He turns back towards us, arms wide to the sky.

"I love life. The melody of it! The whole theme!"

He slowly walks towards the Pacific Ocean without lowering his arms. Monyak distracts me by setting the shot glasses and bottle of Jack back in the Lincoln and gestures for me to get in. I get in the car and watch from the side window as TC disappears from site. I briefly wonder the worst: is he going to kill himself?

"Are we just going to leave?"

Monyak pops the trunk and gets in the car. He opens the divider and hands me about 23 envelopes bounded by a rubber band.

"These are all his poems."

He then hands me a CD.

"All the conversations in this car have been taped."

He closes the divider and hits on the stereo. 'My Way' by Frank Sinatra blares from the trunk. The music is loud, but crystal clear. I look out the window hoping that Ted Christopher reappears into the night. I know he can hear the music, so I can only imagine him standing at the edge of the Pacific, at the edge of darkness and dreaming. The song ends. Monyak closes the trunk, gets in the car and drives away. He takes the Pacific Coast Highway again at break-neck speed. Right now, I spin from the free-flow of booze and cannot catch a coherent thought: a proverbial soup of this and that, sandwiched with more of that and this. By the time I recollect, I find I'm at LAX. He parks at the terminal,

United Airlines. Monyak opens the door. I get out because I felt it was right to, maybe habit.

"Here's a one way ticket back to Cleveland."

He hands me the ticket. I grab the ticket and shake his extended hand.

"Thanks for the ride. It's been interesting. You probably won't answer any of my questions will you?"

"Don't thank me; just follow through... and no."

Monyak gets in the car and rolls down the window.

"Hey kid."

I turn around.

"Here's one more envelope."

I grab the envelope. Its title: MONEY.

"What's this?"

"Eight thousand dollars."

"I can't accept this."

"Yes, you can, kid. He sold his car so you can have it... its just money."

Monyak rolls up the window and drives away. I enter the airport with the strongest will not to elaborate, distinguish, integrate, embellish or even laugh at all that's gone on. I simply and robotically do the charade of getting on a plane and fly. I just fly home.

CHAPTER **23**

ONE LIFE

Months have gone by since I revisited any thought of my disappearance. The winter has re-birthed into spring. Rain pelts my bedroom window and new, random thoughts race through my head. I walk down the outside stairs of my buddy's apartment I so bitingly hate, grab the morning Plain Dealer from a driveway that hasn't had anyone living there for a month, and check out the business page for a quick nugget of the stock market. Why gamble? I peruse the sports edition, just to see how pathetic our baseball team will be this year and close out on the police blotter and the obituaries.

All of a sudden, I freeze, and read about Ted Christopher: he was born on April 23rd and died on April 21st. I laugh from the subconscious surface and think close, very close, but I guess he wasn't Shakespeare. It is strange, but he was strange so it made sense. The obituary did not give the years, it just said he battled the last six months of his life with terminal cancer. I shake my head at my naiveté of missing such an obvious. Everything now makes sense; it's like connecting the dots and figuring out the puzzle. I look to see where the wake is being held and find nothing. It's mysterious, like he didn't even exist. How is anyone going to pay their respects? I close the paper and see the date. It's April 23rd. I run up the outside stairs, stopping at my desk with no chair and pen this: <u>The three keys to life.</u> I look at it and underline it again and again and again. I turn off the stereo, shut off the light and close the curtain. I lie in my bed, fold my hands in prayer upon my chest and listen to the silence. I do not think or move for over an hour: just concentrate on breathing. What was to follow, I cannot fabricate or ever imagine again: I felt my soul. And then, I felt as if my soul was being armored. At this point I realized that there was a God and each one of us is born with a soul. My eyes were closed, and in the darkness, I see a crucifix. The crucifix disappears, becoming a universe of stars. My mind is blank, but conscious at the same time. Suddenly, my eyes twitch uncontrollably, what I imagine to be a deep sleep experience involving rapid eye movement, but I was awake. Then, the universe of stars shoots towards me, as if I was warping through periods of time like being in Star Wars or Star Trek. I just find myself searching for a single star, just a light I can focus upon. That's when it happens, a bright light shot in increments; it begins in my head, shoots through my entire body and exits through my abdominal region. This amazing experience stops, and a few minutes later, my chest begins to rise like a helium balloon. Each breath seems to last about ten minutes. It was as if God himself was giving me the breath of life. I know it sounds crazy, but I felt as if I am Adam in the Garden of Eden. I wanted to go further into this unconscious, but conscious state, but for some reason, I couldn't. As fleeting as it was, I open my eyes, feel my chest and breathe. I truly believe I reached Nirvana. I sit on the edge of my bed and feel radiating warmth flowing to my extremities: complete and happy. I wanted to do something but smoke and drink was quickly erased out as options. I had to do something.

Life seemed to have meaning, beginning now. I jump out of bed, grab a shirt, put on my shoes and run out of the house. I fall into the car and drive to Southpark Mall. I park; I jog through the mall and buy a necklace with a crucifix. I jog through the crowd, to my car, drive down Pearl Rd and into Brunswick. I go to St. Ambrose and enter the Cathedral. I walk down the center of the aisle and kneel down in front of the crucifix and alter and pray. I stand up, make the sign of the cross and walk over to the holy water. I dip the crucifix and put on the necklace. I leave the church and drive down 303 to Resurrection Cemetery in Valley City. I park the car and start walking through the cemetery. I take notice to the names this time. When a person was born and when they died. I just imagine what their time on this earth meant. Did they live a great life? Did they make a difference? All of a sudden, his poems begin to echo in my mind. It was as if he was there, watching me, representing me. The presence is overwhelming. Over and over it echoes in my head: One Life!

I get in my car and start driving; I decide the radio is needed: 'Whole Lotta Love' by Led Zeppelin is playing. The day creeps into night as I veer onto 71 North. I take 480 West without a clue until I see the exit for Clay Park. I look down at the clock: 9:11 p.m. I arrive at Huntington Beach at exactly 9:23. The parking lot is full of cars, full of license plates from all over the United States. I loom at the edge of the steps, looking out at one of the most amazing sites these eyes have ever seen. Hundreds of people occupy the beach, holding white candles, giant speakers line the beach playing: 'A Beautiful Day,' by U2, leading into 'Two Step,' by Dave Matthews Band. I walk down the steps, kick off my shoes and walk barefoot on the sand. I see his best friends: Lewis, Travis, Pat, Mike, John, Ron and Paul in a circle. They pass around a large jug of red wine. I turn away to kegs on the beach and people dancing. It's truly a spectacular, bohemian sight: there are, at least four bonfires blazing and kids running around with sparklers. I walk to the keg, and overhear an older woman whispering to her friend.

"Can you believe it? His family had to shell out the money for this funeral. He died with nothing. He didn't leave anything behind."

I pleasantly grab my beer and restrain from intruding. I shake my head to calm the nerves. There is not enough time in life to argue over what you know is what is true. I start shaking hands and meet his cousins: Dawn, Kelly and Bonnie and his sisters: Terry and Tracy. They all are beautiful, not just physically but in their happy and sincere way of celebrating his life. His older sister wipes away a tear of happiness.

"How did you know my brother?"

"Well, he had a way of changing people's lives without knowing it. He was right. I'm honored to meet all five of you. His family. He always talked about you, guys."

I shake hands with his good friends and continue to walk through the crowd.

The music stops suddenly. A man speaks into the microphone. It's Monyak, reading off an index card.

"Ted Christopher wrote this on the day he died.
The simple poem is titled: THANK YOU

The river flowed through me
The sun shined down on me
The earth moved beneath me
I hold this beauty inside of me
It is surrounding me."

His nephews and nieces lay flowers inside a small boat on the edge of the lake.

"Lay the flowers down on me,"

The candle light vigil gathers around the shore. A flame is being passed from candle to candle. The music of Beethoven's ninth symphony begins to play.

"Say your prayers over me,"

Lewis, Travis, Pat, Mike, John, Ron and Paul carry the small boat into the lake.

"Please God
Please
Let me be found."

His best friends trudge through the dark waters to the point where they can barely breathe. They finally let go of the boat and let it drift away. The best friends walk back on the beach and put their arms around each other's neck.

At this moment, a flash of envy inside my head cascades: this is one hell of a funeral. Five to six men standing on a cliff, overlooking the entire event, start shooting arrows of fire at the boat. A few seconds later, the boat ignites. The music increases in volume as the flames roar high into the sky. The song ends. I decide to walk towards the lake as the music transits to play from the Braveheart soundtrack "Freedom/ The Execution/ Bannockburn," by James Horner. I stand at the water's edge, looking out, smiling at this retrospective rejoice of a man's life. Fireworks begin to explode in the sky. It's like the Fourth of July or, even better, the ending of 'Meet Joe Black.'

"He had passion – so much passion."

I turn around and see a woman in a white sun dress. She holds a white candle. She walks out upon the large stones that lead into the lake. Standing at the edge, she just stares at the moon. I nod my head because I know. I know what the moon is. I walk the stones and approach her.

"Are you Allie?"

She smiles and turns around.

"I am; he's the only one who calls me that name."

I must admit, she is older, but still attractive: so petite, so cute and what a genuine smile, I can see why he loved her.

"I want you to know, that he never stopped talking about you. He gave me this envelope titled Allie and told me not to open it until today. I open the envelope, pull out the letter and read:

ALLIE –MY LOVE

DANCE BAREFOOT
IN THE SAND – IN THE FIELD
MY LITTLE GIRL
MY ALLIE
JUST DANCE
...IN THE MOONLIGHT.

A tear rolls down her cheek. She looks up at the moon.

"The moon, it was ours. He is and will forever be my soul mate."

I look down at water splashing against the rocks and then up at her.

"Allie, I am honored to have met you."

She turns around and gives me a hug. I start to walk away, but for some reason stop.

"He always talked about a masterpiece. Something he had written, or I don't know, a piece of art, a painting or something."

She just laughs.

"That doesn't surprise me."

I shake my head, a habit I picked up from him.

"Would you know where it might be?"

She continues in her enjoyment with a smile.

"If he had a masterpiece, it would be in the basement of 1020 Westchester. It's where he grew up. There's a beam that divides the basement. Just lift the ceiling panels and reach above the beam. It's where he kept his poems; it's where he kept everything close to his heart."

She stands there so confident, looking at me with her smile.

"Thank you, I am so glad I got to meet you."

I turn around and walk back to the beach. I take one last look out into the lake and see that the fire is still burning. I walk the beach towards my car and feel a presence. I whip around back to the lake and see the three women from his bedroom. They are fifteen yards apart and halfway in the lake. The water is waist high. They all stare into the sky. A single star shines bright. I guess some things in life are not meant to be understood. I walk the steps a bit confused, but understand that's what he wanted. I get in my car and drive home.

The next morning, I awake with a sense of freedom. I take a shower, get dressed and grab... a banana. The early morning scent when I walk outside seems fresh and clean as spring should be. I drive, knowing I have a purpose, down 303, down Pearl Road and into Forest Hills, down Magnolia, pass the elementary school and onto Westchester. I pull right up to his childhood home. I am a bit nervous; I sit in the car and look at my reflection in the mirror. My mind races, thoughts begin. Should I go back home? What am I doing here? A voice exclaims: One Life! A kid on a bicycle rides by watching me half the way and turns the corner. I nod and get out of the car to knock on the front door. A woman in her mid-thirties answers the door with her child held tight to her leg. It's too late to turn back now, I have to speak.

"I'm sorry to interrupt your day, but I have a strange favor to ask."

She is hesitant, probably thinks I'm a stalker or something. I just get to the point.

"My friend, Ted Christopher, passed away, he grew up in this house and he told me that he left something in the basement."

She looks down in sorrow and then starts laughing.

"Ted Christopher, he was probably a young kid at the time."

She invites me in and continues to talk, showing me the living room, pointing at the wall.

"My husband and I tore off the wall paper and saw all of this writing. It was Ted mentioning his friends Lewis, Pat, Mike and Paul. So many names, my husband and I just laughed, because he wrote things like being famous and changing the world. It looked great, but we had to throw on the new wall paper."

She leads me down to the basement. I look around and see a pool table, a bar and a piano.

"They left all of the furniture down here. It's still in great condition, so we just kept it." I just look around and think about all the time he spent down here; writing, drinking and playing pool with his friends.

"I'm sorry, but do you mind if I remove some of these ceiling panels."

She picks up her little girl.

"No, go ahead."

I grab a chair and remove some of the panels. I move my hand around and some old beer cans fall from the ceiling. I just look at her and laugh.

"Yeah, I do believe Ted was here."

I continue to search and find a teddy bear and an old prom picture. I dust off the picture and see that it's him and Allie. I must admit, they made a cute couple. I reach back up and find a few notebooks full of writing. I just throw it on the couch below. This is crazy, there's probably an entire life up here. I move the chair over and reach onto the beam and find a full page manuscript. It's bound and ready to read. I knew at this moment that I was holding onto something special. I set the ceiling panels back in place and move the chair back to the table.

"Thank you so much, this is what I came here for."

I grab the picture, the notebooks, the teddy bear and the masterpiece. She leads me outside.

"I never met Ted, but I'm guessing he was a great person."

"He was."

She nods in agreement and closes the door. I drive home.

The front door is wide open. I know it's not a robber; I'm just an idiot in a hurry. I enter the house and walk into my room. I lie on my bed and hold his masterpiece: it's a screenplay titled 'The Struggle of This Life'.

Now I know what I have to do.

'The Struggle of This Life'... is coming.

© Black Rose Writing

Breinigsville, PA USA
13 June 2010
239706BV00003B/2/P